A TOTAL WITCH SHOW

DAKOTA CASSIDY

DAKOTA CASSIDY

ACKNOWLEDGEMENTS

Cover artist: Renee George
Editor: Kelli Collins

AUTHOR'S NOTE

My darling, amazing, stupendous readers,

Thank you for joining me for book fourteen of the Witchless in Seattle Mysteries! Please note, the Witchless in Seattle series is truly best read in order, to understand the full backstory and history of each character as they develop with every connecting book.

Also, please note, I'm prone to taking artistic license with locations and such, and in this book, I've made up some names of prisons and spells and who knows what else. So forgive any places near and dear to your heart in Seattle and surrounding areas if they're not completely accurate or don't actually exist.

Most of all, thank you for continuing to join Stevie, Win and the gang on their adventures—it means the world to me!

Dakota XXOO

CHAPTER 1

"Stephania!" Win bellowed over the howl of the frigid wind. I heard his footsteps pound, even though the slushy ground of February was soft and muddy.

"Boss!" Belfry cried out, the flap of his tiny wings slashing against the air as he rode the wind toward me.

When Win reached me, Whiskey was with him, instantly at my side, lapping at my face and making me giggle, despite my circumstances.

Dropping to his knees, my Spy Guy scooped me up and held me close to his chest, brushing my sopping-wet hair from my forehead.

Even as rain pelted his chiseled face, even though he was soaking wet, he still looked as if he'd fallen from the pages of a magazine.

"Dove? Are you all right? Tell me you're all right," he demanded, running his knuckles over my cheek, making me wince a little at my injuries.

"I'm fine. Just a little banged up and wet."

Belfry landed on Win's shoulder, his tiny face filled with concern. "Boss, what the heck was that?"

I pushed my way to a sitting position and shivered. We'd had record cold weather here in Eb Falls for the past week, and while I love the thought of a cold winter's night by our cozy fireplace in my fuzzy pink bear slippers and velour robe, I don't love when I'm lying flat out on the ground in it.

"Dove, let me help you," Win demanded, lifting me up and carrying me back toward the house where the glow of the interior made me feel safe.

As Win walked up the steps, Whiskey followed, soaked to the bone. I wasn't so much concerned with what had just happened to me, but the mess Whiskey was going to make when he shook the rain from his fur.

I slid out of Win's arms in the foyer and yelled, waving my finger at him with a stern warning, "He's going to make a huge mess all over the floor and walls! We need a towel. We need a dozen towels! Don't you move, Whiskey Cartwright-Winterbottom! Not a muscle!"

As though we were playing a game of freeze tag, Whiskey's tail stopped wagging and he stood stock still. In fact, his tongue was still partially hanging out of his mouth, unmoving.

I gasped in pure shock.

He'd listened to me.

Whiskey hardly ever listens to me. Not in the

history of listening had he ever listened to me. He only listened to Win and Belfry and sometimes Arkady.

Both Bel and Win gave each other strange looks before Win ran to the laundry room to come back with a stack of towels.

He handed me a fluffy white towel. "Come, Dove, let me dry you, you're positively blue."

But I shook my head and took the towel, my teeth chattering. "I can dry myself off. You get Whiskey so he doesn't make the foyer look like Dexter Morgan has been practicing his blood spatter techniques."

Win did as I asked, and still Whiskey didn't move. Not a single muscle.

Belfry buzzed toward me as I dripped all over the entryway carpet, sniffing the air with his tiny snout, his wings moving furiously. "Stevie? You smell that?"

I sniffed the air, too. "You mean the scent of wet dog? I sure do," I muttered, rubbing my arms with the towel.

"No," Bel said, shaking his head with a frown. "That's not it."

As Win knelt and dried Whiskey, he remained frozen, completely immobile. "Whatever in the world is going on?"

I wrapped a towel around my head turban style. "You know, this reminds me of the time I went to my tenth-grade dance with Jake Poloski. He had hands like an octopus. I swear, he was the grabbiest guy I'd ever gone out with. So anyway, we're slow dancing to 'I'll Never Break Your Heart' and he made a grab for a place he knew better than to grab, and I said, 'Don't you move another muscle.' And guess what? He froze. Right there in the middle of the gym dance floor in front of everyone. Just like... *Just like Whiskey,*" I whispered.

"I knew it!" Belfry shouted, circling the room with a squeak of joy. "I knew that's what I smelled!"

Win rose and grabbed a towel for his own hair and began to scrub it dry. "I'm afraid this is a loop I'm not privy to. I don't understand what you smell, mate, or how it relates to Jake and Whiskey. Though, I assure you, if I ever run into this bloke Jake Poloski, I shall show him what the five-fingered death punch is."

I winced, but I was more concerned with why this was happening to Whiskey. Belfry was connecting dots I wasn't. "So what are you smelling, Bel?"

"*Magic*, Boss! he chirped excitedly. "Magic. I smell bonified, real live magic!"

I cocked my head and sniffed the air again. Maybe it had been so long I wasn't able to remember what it smelled like, or maybe Bel had gone quite literally bananas.

"I don't smell it," I said with a dull tone. No way was I going to get my hopes up again only to be crushed like a cracker at the bottom of the box.

Nope. Not this time.

"Then explain Whiskey," he coaxed. "Whiskey and Jake Poloski. Explain them."

I pinched my temples. My head hurt, but I'll get to why later. For the moment, I was stumped. "I can't explain it, Bel. I just said some words. Words I've said a zillion times to Whiskey, and you know how fluky my magic could be back in the early days when I was still learning. Jake was just a product of that." I looked at my sweet dog, drier and fluffier now. "But Whiskey? I didn't do anything special."

Bel sighed and narrowed his tiny eyes at me. "But you did! You were worried Whiskey was going to make a mess, and when Jake got fresh with you at that dance, you were angry. Those emotions sparked your magic."

I rolled my eyes and headed toward the laundry room off the kitchen where I had a bathrobe hanging on a hook. Closing the door, I blew out a breath of air and began pulling my clothes off. "That's baloney and you know it, Bel. I've had tons of glitches before and it's led to absolutely nothing. I make icebergs the size of the Empire State Building in the backyard and then months go by before anything else happens."

"But that wasn't the same, Boss. I didn't smell the magic I'm smelling now. It's different. It's very different."

My heart skipped a beat, but I quelled the butterflies of hope in my belly with a mental stomp.

I refused to get excited over something that never seemed to come to fruition. As I shrugged my arms into my bathrobe, I scoffed. "Baloney on a stick. I'm not going to buy into this nonsense again. Not this time. For now, we need to find out how to help Whiskey."

I popped open the door and found Win and Belfry

now in the middle of the kitchen, where they'd moved a still frozen-in-place Whiskey.

My heart started to thud in my chest. What if it really had been my magic that had done this? How could I fix it?

I bit the nail on my thumb. "What if…what if I can't bring him back? What if he's like this forever?" I asked, hysteria rising in my voice.

Win quickly busied himself making me a hot cup of coffee. "Oh, my Dove, surely you don't think that will happen? How long did Jake the Octopus remain frozen?"

I gulped, tightening the belt of my robe around me and burrowing deep into it as I remembered Ludwig Friedhoff, a German exchange student, and Nelson Riddick carrying his stiff body home to his parents.

"I think it was a couple of days." But I shook my head, letting the towel on my hair fall to the floor. "I can't remember. That was forever ago. The only thing I do remember was the doctor explaining it away as some sort of temporary paralysis. A medical anomaly were his words."

Bel flew to Whiskey's back, landing on his spine. "Well, the scent of the magic wasn't that strong. So you've got that in your favor. I bet you my favorite vacuum clogger will be back to his old self any minute now."

I knelt in the spot where they'd placed Whiskey, wrapping my arms around his neck, tears filling my eyes. "How could this have happened? It's crazy that now, of all times, my magic chooses to work. I'm sorry, buddy."

Win latched onto my upper arm and pulled me upward. "Come now, Mini Spy. We'll figure this out. I promise you. Until then, we have bigger fish to fry."

"I hate fish," I muttered.

"That's not true. You rather enjoy a fish stick sandwich with processed yellow cheese melted on top."

I let him lead me to the table where he set a steaming cup of coffee in front of me. "That's different. It's fake fish."

Win pulled out a chair and grabbed my hand. "Stephania," he said in his uppity British tone, "stop avoiding. Whiskey aside, what just happened out there?"

"I went to get the mail." And that was true. I'd been waiting for two stinkin' weeks for some pillow covers to come and decided it was worth the risk to go to the mailbox and grab them—even in the pouring rain.

"Stephania…" he warned, his handsome face flashing irritation.

"What? I really was going to get the mail. I told you about those pillow covers I ordered, right? The ones with the ruffles that look vintage and French Victorian? They have that sort of worn linen look to them. They're perfect for my bed."

"Did the pillow covers give you the black eye?" Win asked, eyebrow raised, eyes narrowed.

I ran my finger over my very tender right eye. "No,

because they haven't arrived yet. Stupid Pillows Direct. They promised they'd be here a week ago."

Now he sucked in his cheeks—which meant he was super annoyed. "Stephania. Why do you have a black eye and a scraped cheek and who must I hunt down to mete out his punishment?"

If I told Win who socked me in the face and knocked me down, it was going to open a serious can of worms.

Not only that, it wasn't going to make a dang bit of sense.

Belfry flew to the table and crawled up my arm to look me in the eye. "Answer the question, Boss. Who clocked you, at the mailbox of all places?"

I made a face at him. "Who are you? Bad cop? You've been watching too much *On the Case with Paula Zahn.* I'm going to take your Investigation ID channel privileges away."

Now Win's face against the backdrop of our beautiful kitchen looked worried. "Dove, I'm not enjoying this game of cat and mouse. Was it an old lover you're embarrassed over? Someone you didn't tell me about?"

Hah! Because I'd had so many of those. "Don't be ridiculous. I've told you about every date I've ever been on and my broken engagement. Of course it wasn't an old lover."

"You're stalling," he accused, rubbing his thumb over the inside of my wrist.

I looked away from him and out the kitchen bay

window into the dark night, dread flooding my stomach. "I am."

The lines on Win's forehead deepened. "Why, my love?"

"Because it's going to sound crazy," I said, tracing the pattern of the wood on our table.

Win cleared his throat. "Crazier than me reincarnating in my brother's body?"

"Okay, maybe not that crazy." Or maybe it was. I had no clear definition for crazy anymore.

"Please tell me what just happened out there, Stevie."

Blowing out a breath, I gave in. "Okay, so like I said, I was going to check the mail for my pillow covers. It was pouring and a little dark, and I was too stupid to put on a raincoat. The ground was kinda mushy and my feet were getting wet."

My International Man of Mystery clucked his tongue. "I don't need the weather report, Al Roker. I know what it was like outside."

Our mailbox is at the very end of the drive, near the steep road leading to the cliff we live atop, overlooking the water.

"Anyway, just as I was opening the mailbox, someone came up behind me and called my name. I turned around, surprised someone had braved all the rain and wind, and when I said 'that's me,' he said, 'I have a message for you from Sal Finch. He told me to tell you he owes you one and he's coming for you'—and then he popped me in the face and I fell down…and that's what happened."

Everyone sat silent for a moment.

Especially my Whiskey, who still hadn't moved an inch. He almost looked like a stuffed toy.

"Did he mean…Sal Finch, as in my *dead cousin* Sal Finch?"

"Do you know any other Sal who owes me one? I mean, he was kind of my first…kill…I guess you could call it."

I'd come to accept that I'd been a part of someone's death due to the kill-or-be-killed situation, but it didn't make it feel any better. I'd just managed to keep it at bay.

"But Sal is dead," Win refuted.

I wagged a finger at him, my stomach in turmoil. "And if you'll recall, so were you."

CHAPTER 2

*Y*ou might remember Salvatore Finch, Win's cousin, was the original beneficiary on his will, and what started this whole journey.

Win, regretful he'd bequeathed Sal his car and stocks and all the money he'd accumulated, had communicated with Madame Zoltar, asking her to sneak into his lawyer's office and change his will, and that's what had gotten her killed—by Sal.

Who, of course, was infuriated about losing hundreds of millions of dollars to *me*, a total stranger. It's what had begun my relationship with Win five years ago. I said I'd help him find Madam Z's killer.

But you might also remember, Sal died after trying to kill me, as well. So for someone to show up and threaten me with words purportedly from him?

I have to admit, I was a little freaked out.

Win instantly went into spy mode. Sitting up

straight, he called on Arkady. "My friend? Might I speak with you?"

"Dah, Zero. I am always available to you."

I waved up at the ceiling. "How's it going, my sweet blini?"

Arkady sighed with longing. "Arkady miss his country's food, tater tot. Especially blinis. Aside from that, I am well this good night. You? You are not so well. Who give you shiner? I will put hex on them!"

I swallowed hard. "You don't know how to do that and you know it. As for my eyeball, it was someone with a message from Sal."

"Have you heard any rumblings from the afterlife, Arkady? Anything about Stephania or my cousin Sal Finch?" Win asked, his jaw tight, meaning, he was forcing himself to hold it together.

"Nyet, Zero. I hear nothing. Was Sal not my sweet magnolia's first kill?"

"Argh!" I groaned, letting my head fall to my hands. "Don't say it like that. I didn't mean to kill him. He fell. It was an *accident*. You make me sound like a serial killer."

"Ah, yes, sweet dumpling. I forget civilians don't make notches on their bedposts for the pile of bodies they accumulate like we spies do…er, did."

Shivering, I sipped my coffee. "We definitely don't. Well, not normal people, anyway. Serial killers, definitely. But not people who kill out of self-defense. And why are we talking about this? Shouldn't we be worried about someone sending me a message from Sal? Like, *dead* Sal?"

Win rolled his tongue along the inside of his cheek. "Yes. Of course we should, Dove. We should also be icing your eye." He rose to get a bag of peas from the freezer and handed them to me. "Did you get a look at who did this?"

Shaking my head, I wrapped my fingers of my free hand around my mug of coffee, my fingers like ice. "No. He had on a ski mask, but he was about five-ten, and his voice sounded young. Maybe in his early thirties? He had on dark clothes and he wore that awful spray the kids like so much these days. Um…I think it's called Ferocious or something like that. Maybe that's what Belfry smelled," I said on a chuckle.

"Nutter Butters. It was *not* what I smelled," he said petulantly. "It was magic. So suck it. I know magic when I smell it. I'm a familiar, for cripes' sake. I've been smelling it for a trillion years."

"You use magic, chocolate cupcake?" Arkady asked, his voice laced with excitement. "How wonderful for you! It has been many months, no?"

Which was why I wasn't going to get my panties wadded. "No. I mean, yes. It's been months. But I don't know if it was magic…"

"Then explain Whiskey," Belfry demanded. "Look at him, Arkady. Frozen in place. How did that happen if not for magic? I don't have any magic and neither does Winterbutt."

Poor Whiskey, sitting in the middle of the kitchen,

looking like he'd just returned from the taxidermist, made me want to curl up in a ball and cry.

"Belfry is right. Why else does this happen, my *malutka*?"

Instead of crying, I went with angry. I was angry Whiskey was a victim of my hapless magic. "I can't explain it, but I *can* tell you if he can't be fixed, I swear I'm going to hunt Baba Yaga down at one of her stupid eighties parties and shred every last one of her pairs of leg warmers, then set them on fire and roast Twinkies over them!"

Win's eyes narrowed. "Ah, yes, the beautiful Baba Yaga."

Yes. The beautiful, ageless, stuck-in-the-'80s fearless leader who'd kicked me out of my coven instead of listening to my side of the story.

She'd shunned me. I thought I was over it, but I guess I wasn't *totally* over it, because it still niggled at me a little. "I'll *make* her fix him if I have to."

Belfry tucked himself against my ear. "Calm down, Boss. We'll figure Whiskey out. Until then, we need to figure out your magic and this Sal thing."

I cupped my chin in my hand. "Let's focus on Sal. How could Sal possibly get a message to me through someone else? How did he convince someone else to do it and to punch me in the face? Wouldn't Sal have to possess him to get him to do what he wants?"

As I held the package of peas against my throbbing eyeball, Win said, "Possession seems to rather be the rage these days, doesn't it? I feel like everyone but me has mastered possession."

"But wait. Before we jump to possession, did he possess him or did he just whisper a *suggestion* in his ear?" I wondered. "I mean, that's pretty common. You know, devil on one shoulder, angel on the other, that sort of thing? He probably didn't cross over. He's likely on one of the other planes. Now that would make sense."

"I thought the angel/devil concept was simply your conscience talking?"

"Sometimes it is. And sometimes it's a spirit."

"Either way, it still means someone wants you harmed, and I won't have it." He tightened his fists.

Win's protectiveness when it came to me always made my heart warm and my toes tingle. "Maybe it was just a prank?" I suggested with hope in my words, setting the bag of peas down.

"Who, after all this time, is even thinking of Sal Finch? It feels like ages ago since he almost killed you, Stephania."

I wish my head felt the same way. It still ached sometimes where he'd cracked me but good. "I don't know, but kids will be kids. Maybe it was some kind of hazing or something. Like the high school kids had to do something to the psychic lady who killed a guy."

"Bah! That's ridiculous. You said he looked like he was in his thirties. Regardless, I have to doubt a hazing would involve punching you in the face, Dove. Scaring you? Maybe. Taking something of yours that's personal? Maybe. But all the children at the school love you. They think you're—"

"Snatched, which means cool," Bel interjected. "None of them would ever hurt you. Nah, something's brewing, I can feel it in my bones, Boss, and it has to do with your magic. Remember I said those words."

Just then, Whiskey's tail fluttered, and then he was all sound and motion, jumping into my lap and licking my face.

I threw my arms around him and hugged him hard, burying my face in his thick fur. "Oh, thank the goddess you're all right! I never would have survived this if something happened to you. I love you, buddy."

Just as he was about to lavish my face with more wet kisses, he suddenly reared back and looked at me as though he'd never seen me before in his life.

I frowned, my heart thumping in my chest. "Whiskey? What's the matter, pal?"

He sniffed the air around me, smelling my drying hair and the skin on my arms before he jumped off my lap and ran to hide behind Win's chair, almost cowering from me.

What the heckadoodles was going on?

"He smells it, too," Belfry remarked cockily. "He smells your magic."

No, no, no. I wasn't buying into this. "Oh, he does not, Bel. Maybe I smell like the guy who socked me in the face?"

"Let's bring Spike in and see what he thinks," Bel

suggested. "Animals have a sixth sense about these things. Win, do you mind getting the door?"

Obviously Win knew Bel was trying to prove a point, but he didn't want to hurt me—or at least the look he gave me suggested as much.

I waved a hand. "Go ahead."

Win opened the French doors that led to Spike's outdoor cage, where he sat under a heat lamp. Sometimes he seemed to enjoy spending time alone, so we'd made sure he had a space of his own that connected to the house.

"Spike!' I called. "Gobble, gobble, punkin'! Mama's got treats."

I don't know if he really understood the bit about me having treats or even what I was telling him. But he did know the sound of my voice and he always responded.

He came waddling into the kitchen as I rose to get him some dried cranberries, which he adored. Pouring some in my hand, I held them out to him and he ran toward me, stopping just shy of the tips of my fingers.

"Look, bud. Cranberries! They're your favorite." I wiggled my fingers with a smile, but his webbed feet took a couple of steps backward before he turned tail (or is that feather?)—and made a run for a spot behind Whiskey.

"I don't understand," I whispered, my shoulders sagging in defeat as tears filled my eyes.

If it were true, if this was my magic, and it meant

Whiskey and Spike wouldn't come near me, I didn't want it. Baba Yaga and the coven could keep it.

"Well, I guess you made your point, Bel. Happy?"

"Oh, my sweet *malutka*, I am hugging you right now. Little man means no harm. He is only trying to help."

Bel buzzed to my shoulder and tucked himself against my ear, his soft fur soothing me. "He's right. I'm just trying to help. It's gonna be okay, Stevie B. They'll get used to you again. I promise. But they have to get to know the new you, that's all."

My eyes filled with tears, the sore eye stinging. "But I'm not new, Belfry! I'm the same old Stevie who was thrown out of her coven like week-old leftovers after basically being called a liar. The same one who made a new life for herself—from scratch, mind you—in her hometown, where everyone thought she was a murderer! I'm *that* Stevie. I'm not Stevie the witch anymore. I'm not."

Win held out a hand to me, his handsome face pained, his crisp ice-blue shirt still wet from the rain. "Dove, please. Let's sit and talk this through, the way we always do."

But I didn't know *what* I wanted to do. Secretly, for months upon months after losing my powers, I'd prayed to the goddesses—begged them to give me my witch powers back, to let me back into the coven. For someone, *anyone*, to show up and let me go back to my old life in Texas.

But that never happened. So I started over, and now my life was good. Really, really good. Better than it was in Texas. I had friends here. People who were loyal to me, unlike my coven, with the exception of Winnie.

And then there was Win. We had a life, a home I loved. He had the garden society, his friendships with Dana and Sandwich, and I had Madam Zoltar's, and Arkady, and my own friendships with various business owners in Eb Falls.

I didn't want that to change, and being a witch again *would* change it. It would change everything. They'd want me to come back to the coven, and I wasn't going back to a place where everyone had betrayed me.

"No!" I yelled into the kitchen. "I don't want to talk about this. There was a time when I would have given almost anything to have my magic back. For Baba Yaga to believe in me—stand behind me when Adam West-field did what he did. But she didn't, and I had to start a new life, and I'm happy now. I don't want to be a witch anymore. I just want to be Stevie Cartwright from Ebenezer Falls, Washington, who can see ghosts and is going to marry Crispin Alistair Winterbottom and live happily ever after in their mini-mansion. End of."

Win wrapped his strong arms around me and pressed a kiss to the top of my head, pulling me close. "Oh, my sweet Dove. Being a witch is part of who Stevie Cartwright is, no matter how much you wish it weren't so."

Bel buzzed to his shoulder and nodded his fluffy head. "He's right, Boss. No matter what that fruitcake Adam did, you'll always be a witch."

I pushed away from Win, despite the warmth his arms brought me, panic setting in. "Fine. I can be a witch all you want, but if I *am* a witch again, if my powers are returning, I'm not going back to the coven in Texas. *I won't.* I'm not leaving Eb Falls."

"Now, Boss—"

"I said no!" I yelped like a petulant child, and when I did, quite suddenly, The Backstreet Boys were standing in the middle of my kitchen.

The *Backstreet Boys.*

CHAPTER 3

I blinked and then I blinked again. "Is that… are they…?"

"The Backstreet Boys, Boss? Yep. Every last one of 'em. Like they were cryogenically frozen, doing whatever it was they were doing before you zapped 'em here."

"But…how did I…?"

Bel flew around Kevin Richardson (who was dressed in the cutest pair of pajamas ever. Flannel and checkered. Who knew? Phew, he was as cute up close as he was from afar) and chirped, "I don't wanna say anything, but it might be your magic. Just sayin'."

I'd swoon, but I couldn't move. I almost couldn't breathe. *Kevin Richardson* was standing right in front of me. I could see his every pore, see every whisker on his chin.

He was so dreamy…

But why would my magic summon, of all things, the

Backstreet Boys? That made no sense. Whiskey's frozen state sort of made sense in correlation to Jake, but a boy band?

Win circled the men, hands in his trouser pockets, cheeks hollow from sucking them inward. "So these are the men you're always fawning over? The ones who screech like cats being skinned on that setlist you have on Spotify?"

I made a face. "Well, fawn is a big word. Maybe more like admire," I replied coolly.

My heart raced as I stared at Nick Carter in jeans and a holey T-shirt, his blond hair ruffled, his eyes so blue I thought I might fall into them like a pool of glistening water.

"Admired, schmadmired. You were in love with Kevin and you know it. You bought every magazine he was ever in. You had posters of him on your walls, and one you even kissed good night every single night for a year before you went to bed."

My cheeks flamed hot. "I was only eleven or twelve, for cripes' sake, Bel. Stop revealing all my childhood secrets!"

Win put his hands on Kevin's shoulders. "Is this the beloved boy-singer Kevin?"

I looked down at my feet and shrugged, fighting a grin. "Maybe. Are you a little jealous, International Man of Mystery?"

Arkady began to laugh, deep and hearty. "Zero, the look on your face is without price."

"I most certainly am not. But I can assure you, he's

never hung from the side of a mountain with shark-infested waters below him while chasing a world-renowned arms dealer," Win mumbled.

I put my hands behind my back and chuckled, giving him a smug face. "He kind of didn't have to. He was busy singing to sold-out stadiums to millions of swooning teenagers. Now stop being jelly and help me figure out how to get them back to whatever it was they were doing. Obviously, Howie was in the middle of his dinner." I grabbed a paper napkin from the counter. "He has spaghetti sauce on the corner of his mouth." I gently wiped it away, my pulse racing.

I was actually *touching* Howie Dorough! Boy, did he smell good. I had to fight to keep my knees from melting.

AJ must have been preparing to go out, sleek in a burgundy suit and tie, and Brian, whose eyes were as blue as Nick's, was dressed as casually as Nick. Simple jeans and a T-shirt, with some sneakers.

I had to move away from them. I couldn't stand near Kevin or I'd fall apart. Bel had been right. I'd been madly in love with him at one time and had planned our magical wedding at least a hundred different ways. Being so close to him was surreal.

But that still didn't explain how they'd gotten here.

"So how do we send pretty boys back to home?" Arkady asked.

I swallowed hard. That part of it worried me. What if I couldn't get them back where they belonged? "I don't know, Arkady. I don't know how they got here in the first place."

"Maaagic!" Belfry sang. "You were angry, and earlier you were talking about Jake Whatshisface and the tenth-grade dance. You were slow-dancing to a Backstreet Boys song when he got fresh, right?"

I gripped the counter, trying not to allow the panic of my wildly out-of-control magic take over. "Yes. I did say that."

Bel flew to my face. "It's your emotions, Stevie. They're all out of whack right now, but you can control them if you just try. Once you calmed a bit, Whiskey came back, right?"

My dog was still cowering behind Win. "Well, yeah, but he hates my guts. I'm not sure I could take Whiskey *and* the Backstreet Boys hating my guts."

"Stevie, don't be a derp. Whiskey doesn't hate your guts. He's confused. He just smells you differently now. You're like a new person, that's all. Now get it together and stop complaining. Take a deep breath and think about sending the pretty boys back to their families."

I thought about that for a minute. They could always stay for dinner. Sure, it'd be a little weird at first, but Win's so charming, he'd win them over.

"Do I have to?"

I mean, c'mon. How often does a girl get the boys of her prepubescent dreams in her kitchen all at once?

"You do, indeed, *Dove,*" Win said from a tight jaw.

I chuckled. Win was even cuter when he was jealous. "Okay, okay."

"Now take a deep breath and clear your mind of everything but sending the boy-toys back home," Bel instructed as he flew to Kevin's shoulder and sat on it.

"Fine, but we have plenty of room, you know," I protested. "They could all stay here."

"Not today, young lady," Bel chastised while Arkady snickered.

Closing my eyes, I thought about how much the Backstreet Boys' families would miss them and how sad their children would be if they weren't there, and when I popped my eyes back open, they each shimmered…and then they were gone.

Bye-bye, Kevin. I'll always remember our time together, even if you won't.

Bel and Arkady cheered, but Win obviously saw how defeated I looked.

"Dove? Are you all right?" he asked, his handsome face fraught with worry.

Sighing, I decided I was being a whiny baby and maybe I needed a shower and some alone time before dinner.

Standing on tiptoe, I pressed a kiss to his cheek. "I'm fine, Win. Really. I just need a hot shower and a moment to myself. You okay with that?"

He pressed a kiss to my lips. "Of course, my love. How about I order in, yes? Maybe something from that new French place? They deliver. Some beef bourguignonne sound good?"

I nodded and squeezed his arm. "That sounds great."

"I'll pop the cork on that red wine we grabbed while we were there the last time, and you'll feel better in no time."

I started to make my way toward the stairs. "Okay. Thanks, guys. I'll be down in a bit."

Traipsing up the steps, sad my shadow Whiskey wasn't following me the way he usually did, I headed straight for my bathroom with its freestanding oval tub and its beautiful marble sink, and I turned on the water as high as it would go to cover the sound of my sobs.

No, I wasn't crying over the Backstreet Boys having to leave, though, it was a good thing I wasn't twelve or there'd have been legendary hysterics.

I was crying because of Whiskey and Spike. I was crying because I felt in my gut—in my soul—that my life was about to drastically change, and I didn't want that.

I didn't know if the change would be about me getting my magic back, or it was something else.

I only knew I didn't want whatever it was.

I didn't want it at all.

Win poured me a glass of wine and I took a huge gulp, toying with my beef bourguignonne from Juliette's. Tender and delicious, I love the beef and carrots, but my appetite was almost nonexistent.

He'd changed into a light blue sweater and a pair of

black trousers, looking as though he'd never been outside in the pouring rain. He reached for my hand and caressed it with his thumb. "Can I butter you a piece of that crusty baguette you so enjoy? You know how much you love it. I had Juliette put in an extra loaf for us. You can have the leftovers for breakfast with that godawful store-bought apricot jam you so treasure," he enticed.

"Thanks, Win. You're the best fiancé a girl could ask for."

"Better than Kevin?" he teased as he buttered a thick slice of bread and handed it to me.

"I don't know. I think I need to see you in a pair of plaid pajamas and get engaged to him before I decide," I half-heartedly joked.

He grinned, those deep grooves on either side of his mouth standing out. "I shudder at the mere thought of those pajamas."

Win wore silk pajamas, and only the bottoms, his strong, incredibly sexy chest remaining uncovered when he slept. I'd caught a peek at him once when he'd left his cell phone at the house. If you're wondering, I didn't leave disappointed.

He was still staying in our decked-out guesthouse and planned to do so until we married, to keep tongues from wagging. I told him in this day and age, no one cared, but he reminded me that some of the ladies of the garden club cared, and they reminded him often to stay on the straight and narrow.

Biting into the chewy-soft bread, I thought about

what my attacker said right before he knocked me in the kisser. Sal owed me one…that part, I got. I had sort of killed him.

But *he* was coming for me? How the you-know-what was he going to do that?

It had taken Win months to possess a body, and he wasn't exactly a weak man. His ghostly skills had been quite impressive. But Sal was an idiot.

How was he going to "come for me" unless he meant to haunt me? Which wouldn't be so hard if he found the right connections on whatever plane he'd ended up on—especially due to my connection to the afterlife.

"Tell me, my sweet Dove, why are you so reluctant to have your powers back? You appear almost vehement about the idea. I understand you've become adjusted to this life, and your life is a happy one, but being a witch is part of who you are. You told Dana that yourself. You even threw down the gauntlet and told him to accept you as you are or move along. Talk to me about how you're feeling. What is it you fear?"

I *had* said that to Dana, and it was true. Being a witch was part of who I am, but I'd *become* something more than my powers. I'd grown into a different person.

Shrugging, I took a sip of the delicious wine. "I fear resentment toward my coven. Not a single soul stood by me but Winnie and Bel. *No one*. That was a bitter pill to swallow because it means our alliances, our friendships, weren't as deep as I'd thought."

"But surely they feared the wrath of Baba Yaga should they contact you? Surely they feared a similar fate to yours as outcasts?"

A tear stung my eye. "Winnie didn't…"

Win nodded with a slow bounce of his head. "A fair assessment."

It might be fair, but saying the words aloud made me realize how selfish it was to ask my coven to risk the lives of their families in order to save me. I can't say I wouldn't have done the same.

Yet…The betrayal still felt very real.

"But it isn't just that," I insisted "They'll want me to come back to Texas. They'll want me to join them again to keep the coven strong, and I don't want to leave my life here, Win, or our house—or you."

"Should you choose that path, surely I can go back with you?"

I grabbed his hand and tried to visualize Win in the Texas heat with a cowboy hat. "Yes. Yes, you could go back with me. But would you want to leave the life we've built here, Win? The house, the garden club. Dana and your rugby dates, Sandwich, Chester?"

His blue eyes softened and he smiled. "I would if I were with you."

I leaned over the dining room table and kissed him square on the lips, cupping his chin with my hand. "You really are the best, but it's not what I want. No one wanted me when I was weak and helpless, but they'd sure want me if my powers returned." I paused a moment before I said, "You know what? I almost hope my magic never comes back. Yes, being a witch is—or *was*—who I am, but I'm also a medium, a business owner, a dog and turkey mom, a friend and a fiancée. All those things are here in Eb Falls."

"Here's something to think about, what about your sister Hal, in Maine? She's not part of a coven and no one is pressuring her to be a part of one."

Covens were intricate business, some more intricate than others. "Not all covens are the same. There are plenty of witches who live solitary lives outside of covens, and then there are covens like mine, who like for you to stick close."

Win wiped his mouth with a napkin and looked thoughtful for a moment. "What of Dita? Your mother? She doesn't live in Texas."

I snorted. "For all the changes my mother's made in her life recently, it doesn't make up for the shenanigans she managed when she was part of the coven when I was a child. They weren't sad to see her leave, believe me. But the minute I could leave Eb Falls, I did, and they welcomed me with open arms. Until they didn't."

Win sighed. "I hate that you're so torn, Dove, but wherever you go, know I'll always go with you. *Always.*"

I looked around at our kitchen, remembering the disaster this house had been when I first took Win up on his offer to find Madam Z's killer and live in what we had once called Mayhem Manor.

I honestly thought the entire place would have to be mowed over by a wrecking ball, but with time and

Win's meticulous eye for detail, he'd turned it into a magical place.

Now it was beautiful, with white marble countertops and white cabinets, the beautiful shiplap on the wall in the dining area, the Italian blue and white tiles behind the stove and the pizza oven.

It felt like home. My home. *Our* home. So if Bel had smelled magic, if Whiskey and Spike were afraid of me because my scent had changed, they'd just have to get used to it, because I wasn't leaving here.

"Boooossssss!" Bel called out as he flew in from outside, something hanging from his wing. It swung wildly as he soared into the kitchen and landed on the table, his fur wet.

I grabbed my napkin to dab at his fur and asked, "What's going on, bud?"

"Look what I found out by the mailbox!" he said, his tone full of pride.

I looked down at the table to see what looked like an ID card. Picking it up, I flipped it over and read, "Larch County Corrections. Security Enforcement Officer. Dale Rainwater."

"Larch County Corrections?" Win said. "Isn't that where Charles, your stepfather Bart's son, got life for killing his father?"

A few years back, my mother Dita had come to show off her newest husband Bart at our housewarming party, having no idea he'd end up dead and his son—half warlock, with visions he'd spent all his life trying to understand...a son Bart never knew existed—would kill him.

And suddenly, clear as day, like a bolt of thunder zapping me, I'll never forget as the police took Charles away, how he'd screamed, *"He's coming for you, Stevie, and he's going to make your death a living Hell!"*

Um, eep.

CHAPTER 4

"Maybe Dale Rainwater is Charles's security guard? Do they assign certain people to prisoners? How does that work?"

"No, Dove. In most cases that's not how it works. Though, I'm certain there are some guards better with temperamental inmates than others, but what I fear you're saying is somehow Sal got through to Charles, and Charles passed the message onto Dale, yes?"

My lips thinned. "It makes sense. Otherwise, why would Sal choose Dale, a stranger, to pass on a message? The same message Charles had passed on to me not long ago? So yes. I think Sal has weaseled his way into Charles's head, and Charles, passed the message on to Dale."

Win looked thoughtful for a moment. "I thought your Baba Yaga was going to take care of him? Surely, if he has powers, he shouldn't be with the general population? He could wreak all manner of havoc."

"She disabled his powers."

"She can do that?" Win asked in wonder.

Baba Yaga… Just her name was making me angry right now. "She can. They weren't terribly strong to begin with due to the fact that he was labeled a troublemaker and no one ever taught him otherwise because no one knew he was half warlock. But she can't stop someone from getting into someone *else's* head if she's not aware. If Sal got into Charles's ear, which is how I think poor Dale got involved, who knows what he said."

Win peered out the windshield at the gray day. "That makes perfect sense. Charles and this prison are the only connection to Dale and you."

"Exactly. It was a roundabout way to go about it, but it's the most plausible answer. Plus, Dale said exactly what Charles said to me that night he was arrested, and I'm betting Sal's taking great pleasure in reminding him."

"Thus Sal is using Charles and Dale."

I ran my finger along the vinyl of the seat and nodded. "Likely."

We sat for a moment, silent and contemplative before Win said, "You do, of course, realize you'll never get inside the prison, don't you, Dove? As lovely and charming as you are, you must be on an approved list, especially when one is in maximum security."

I sat in the passenger seat of my car and gave my handsome beloved a cocky smile. "Said the spy who managed to get into Buckingham Palace."

He gripped the steering wheel, his strong hands flexing, one eyebrow raised. "So you're going to scale the prison walls with rope and spiked shoes to get inside?"

I studied my cute flared jeans and black-heeled boots. I was so proud of this outfit due to the fact that in total, it had cost ten dollars, that's including the herringbone blazer.

"I'll do no such thing, and I'm not scaling anything, Tom Cruise. I'm just waiting for Dale's shift to be over and then we're going to have a chat about why he'd punch me in the face, then tell me Sal owed me one and that he's coming for me. How does he even know Sal? It *has* to be through Charles, who's still an inmate. Unless Sal was in prison here in the states or he knew Dale somehow?" I turned to look at Win. "I mean, do you know anyone named Dale Rainwater—any relation to you, per chance?"

Win gave me a grim look. "No, Mini-Spy. No one I know, and Sal had no prison record here in the states that I'm aware of."

I clutched the card that identified Dale as a security officer and cocked my head. "Maybe he *is* related to you and you don't know it. It's not like that hasn't happened before. Might I remind you of your brother Balthazar? Your *twin*? You didn't know he existed." I held the card in front of his face. "Look again. Don't you see the resemblance around the eyes?" I teased.

Dale looked nothing like Win. Round-faced and dark-eyed, with a doughy double chin, he was the antithesis of Win—even as cheerful and pleasant as he appeared in his picture.

He chuckled his deep laugh. "Oh, Dove. Ever a delight. While it's true I'm adopted, and I know little about my biological family, I highly doubt Dale and I are of relation. Also, I can't promise I won't throttle him. He *hit* you. With his fist. I absolutely won't have such violence directed at my beloved."

I reached upward to pull the car's visor down and looked in the mirror. I really had a shiner, but I've had worse in my time. I'd managed to cover most of it with makeup, but it still stung like nobody's business.

"You'll do no such thing. Do you want to end up sitting next to Charles for life if things get out of hand? We're just here to talk to Dale and return his ID card. I'm sure he's been looking for it."

Win turned to me, his black leather jacket crinkling. "Do you really believe Dale was under the influence of some evil spirit, Stephania? Really? If neither Sal nor Charles have any powers, how is that possible?"

I nodded. The more I'd thought about it last night as I tossed and turned, the more I suspected that was the case. Why would some absolute random stranger come to my house, threaten me so specifically, then hit me? There were other forces at work here, and if what Belfry said about smelling magic was true, maybe Sal was trying to reach me. Sal the malevolent.

"I don't know. I only know, it's not as hard as you think to get a message through. You know that yourself."

"Then I shall keep my hands in my pockets, but I make no promises there won't be carnage should the opportunity present itself. One wrong word and he'll never forget he met Crispin Alistair Winterbottom."

I patted his thigh and smiled. "Please remember your name is Christoph Alexander Winningham these days. Now, hush and behave."

I thought of what I'd learned about Dale so far. I'd looked him up on Facebook, and while his profile wasn't public, I could see a few facts.

Dale liked to bowl, shoot pool, and he liked a craft beer from time to time. He enjoyed tending his herb garden and was especially proud of the rosemary he'd grown this past year. He had a cat named Brenda, a little black and orange tortie who appeared to adore him, if the zillion pictures of her said anything about their relationship.

His musical interests lie in the grunge/punk rock area, he liked sci-fi shows and psychological thrillers, and he was, according to him, happily single.

And as far as I was concerned, none of that added up to him being violent enough to sock me in the face last night.

"Look." I pointed to the exit on the left side of the institutional-looking façade, where men and women in uniforms began to pour out of the building. "The shift is ending. Dale should be coming out any minute."

Win sighed. He wasn't thrilled about confronting Dale Rainwater in the first place, so I expected nothing less. "I'm not overjoyed about this idea. I think we should call his superiors and report him."

"And say what? Dale brought me a message from a dead guy then punched me in the face?"

Win shook his head. "You have a point. I have to say, I'm impressed with how you found out which shift he worked, Stephania. You're becoming quite the spy."

I smiled at him, but then my cheek hurt from my shiner and I had to stop. "It wasn't hard. A friend sent him a post last week, asking if he wanted to grab a beer when his shift was over at three."

"Still, your eye for detail is becoming finely honed."

I heard the pride in his voice and it made me blush. I loved Win more every day, and his pride in me made me happy. I thought working together, living next to one another, being together almost 24/7, would put undue strain on our relationship, but since we'd worked out how we solved crimes together and found our roles, it had been pretty great.

My phone buzzed a text then. I pulled my phone from my purse. "Shoot, I forgot about Sandwich."

"Sandwich?" Win asked. "What about him?"

"He likes a giiiirl," I sang with a smile. "He asked if he could talk to me about it and I said yes. But it'll have to wait for now."

As we watched the men and women leave the building in their dark blue uniforms, I spotted Dale immediately. He lumbered toward a new-ish green Ford Focus, a lunch pail under his arm.

I hopped out of the car and called his name. "Dale? Dale Rainwater?"

He stopped just as he opened the car door, squinting into the gray, hazy day. "Yeah?"

I zipped around cars until I reached his, holding up the card. "I think I have something that's yours."

The first thing I noted, he didn't appear to recognize me at all. And I do mean *at all*. There are actors and then there are actors, and he certainly didn't qualify as an Academy Award nominee. He looked at us like any total stranger would, curious but blankly.

Then I saw relief in his eyes and he smiled, his round face scrunching up, his eyes almost swallowed by his red cheeks. "Holy spit!" he called out. "Thank you! Thank you so much, Miss…?"

I smiled and handed it to him, feeling Win come up behind me, his hand at my waist. "Cartwright. Stevie Cartwright."

He clung to the ID as though it were the reason he breathed. "Aw, Miss Cartwright, you have no bloomin' idea the kind of what-for I got from my boss this morning for losing this. It's a lot of changing things in the computer and access codes and a whole rigamarole no one wants to go through. We're supposed to guard these with our lives. Guess I didn't do a very good job of it, huh?" He leaned against the doorframe of his car and looked at us. "Where the heck did you find it?"

Win and I looked at each other. Dale Rainwater appeared so surprised to see his ID card and us, I think we were as caught off guard as him.

Thus, as I approached the subject, I was cautious. "You don't remember me, Mr. Rainwater?"

His eyes went a little dark and a little suspicious. "Do you work at the pet store? That was the last time I remember seeing it. I went to get my girl Brenda her special food. She has trouble with her digestion. I left work yesterday, went to the pet store and went home to catch the hockey game."

Win's cheeks sucked inward, one of those sure signs he was growing impatient. "I assure you, Miss Cartwright does not work at the pet store."

Now Dale's light suspicion went dark and heavy as he frowned. "Well, ain't you Mr. Snooty? If you don't work at the pet store, where'd you get it? Are you one of those groupies who hang around here, hoping to get in to see a murderer?"

"Are you familiar with Charles Rawlings? He's a prisoner here."

He blew out a breath, his cheeks puffing outward. "You *are* one of those crazy groupies. Listen, I can't give you any information on prisoners. You'll have to read the Internet or whatever you crazies do to get in to see these guys."

"But you do know Charles," I pressed.

His eyes narrowed, cold and annoyed. "I don't know anything or anyone. So thanks for my ID card, but I gotta go. I don't have time for this kinda nuttiness."

Well, that was that, eh? He wasn't going to share sensitive information, meaning it was best to move on.

Also, Win was going to lose his cool if I didn't intervene. I put a hand on Win's arm and said, "No, Mr. Rainwater. I'm not a groupie. I know of Charles Rawlings because I watch the news. And I don't work at a pet store, though I wouldn't hate a job like that. I found your ID at my house. I live in Ebenezer Falls. Does that sound familiar?"

He looked at me as though I'd grown ten feet and sprouted hair on my face. "I've never even been to Ebenezer Falls."

"Then you don't remember meeting my fiancé last night at our home, near our mailbox?" Win asked, his tone tight and terse.

As people wandered past us, giving Dale strange looks, he became even more uncomfortable. A bead of sweat formed on his upper lip and he drove his hands into his pockets. "Look, I don't know who you nutballs are, but I've never been to Ebenezer Falls, and I definitely haven't been to your house. I've never seen neither one of you before in my life! What kinda game are you playin' here?"

His voice rose as his panic began to seep outward. Still, I tried to behave as calmly as I could and not attract any more attention. "We're not playing a game, Mr. Rainwater. You *were* at our house in Ebenezer Falls last night. You brought me a message from someone."

He made a face of absolute horror and distaste. "First I lost my ID card at your house, and now I brought you a message. What kind of crackpots are you? What do you want from me?" he yelped, making a few of his colleagues stop nearby.

"Not only did you bring Miss Cartwright a message, but you did this to her eye." Win pointed an accusatory finger at my face.

Aw man! He'd done it now. Win did exactly what he always told me not to do. Don't become emotionally involved.

Compartmentalize, Stephania. Compartmentalize.

We weren't going to get a dang thing out of him now.

Now Dale Rainwater wasn't only angry, but freaked out as he looked around surreptitiously to see who was watching. "I dang well did not hit a lady! Are you bananas? I would never hit a lady. *Never.* You people are trying to start trouble where there ain't any, and I don't know what you want, but you ain't gonna get it here. Now go away and leave me the frack alone!"

I gave Win my displeased, "shut up, thank you very much" look. Turning back to Dale, I tried to soothe him. "Please, Mr. Rainwater, hear me out. I'm not here to accuse you of anything. I'm here to understand. Are you sure you don't remember seeing me in Ebenezer Falls?"

He gave me another shocked look, his pudgy face scrunching up. "You just said I hit you, lady! I'd say that's an accusation. I can't have a thing like that floating around. I'm a security guard at a prison. My reputation is stellar. I won't let you ruin it!"

"I didn't accuse you of hitting me, *he* did." I pointed a finger at Win, throwing him directly under the bus for breaking the rules because he sure as heck wasn't compartmentalizing.

"Lady?" A tall, lanky man with unusually muscular arms and a lean waist approached us, standing in front of Dale, who was obviously well-liked by his peers. "I don't know who you are, or who your fancy guy here is, but Dale would never hit anyone. Now, you're causing a real scene, and it's not the time or place. I think you'd better get in your little toy car and go on home. If Dale hit you, the best thing for you to do is file a police report and call our superiors."

As a crowd began to gather, Win said, "Do pardon me," he flipped the man's ID card attached to his shirt by a clip upward with two fingers and squinted at his name, "*Leonard*, but we're not here to speak with you. This man accosted my fiancée, of that I'm sure. So I'll kindly ask once—and if you value your safety, you'll take heed—for you to please move along and let us speak with Mr. Rainwater."

Holy spumoni, I was going to kill him. I ground the heel of my boot into his shiny leather shoe and grabbed him by the arm. "We're sorry to have bothered you, Mr. Rainwater, but if you remember anything about our meeting, please call me." I pulled a card out of my purse and held it out to him.

Leonard grabbed it, his jaw tight as I pulled Win back toward our *toy car*. "Get in the car before I show you what I know about the five-fingered death punch!" I hissed at him.

He slid into the driver's side soundless, and with the entire parking lot staring at us, drove away.

I was so angry, I wanted to stop the car, jump out, drag him out with me, and challenge him to a mud wrestling fight. I didn't even have words for how angry I was. And to think, I was only moments ago pontificating about how well we worked together.

We sat silent for at least half an hour on the highway before I could even consider speaking.

"What was that about, Crispin Alistair Winterbottom?" I demanded as the gray day rushed past us.

"I recall you reminding me, it's Christoph Alexander Winningham now."

"Don't you play semantics with me, Spy Guy! What was that about back there? What happened to compartmentalization and keeping your emotions out of an investigation?"

He sighed, looking positively defeated, very unlike Win. "I know, I know. I lost my cool. It's not something I do very often, but seeing the face of the man who clobbered you, looking at you as though he'd never seen you before in his life, incited me to behave poorly. My deepest apologies."

I loosened the grip on the handle of my purse, my eyeball throbbing, suddenly feeling badly for being so angry when he'd done what he'd done out of love.

But then I wondered, "Didn't you fight battles with Miranda and other spies all the time? Your emotions didn't get the better of you then, did they?"

"Quite honestly, Dove, I didn't love Miranda the

way I love you. Also, you're not as skilled as Miranda was at handling a situation."

I ignored the part about how I didn't go to spy school and focused on the fact that he loved me more than he had Miranda. "Then let's let it go. But please don't do it again. We got nowhere because you scared him."

He reached for my hand and kissed the tips of my fingers, sending tingles along my spine. "Forgive me?"

I squeezed his hand. "Yes. Of course, I forgive you. So let's forget about that and discuss the blank look on Dale's face when he saw us. It was freaky-deaky. I mean, he had to know what I looked like so he'd sock the right person in the face, right? But it didn't look like he knew who I was at all."

"It was as though you were a complete stranger."

"So you believed him when he said he didn't have a clue who I am?"

"I did. Didn't you?"

Folding my hands in my lap, I looked out the windshield and nodded. "I did, and it weirded me out. But that says to me there are afterlife hijinks at play here. Someone's been in Dale's ear. How they did it, I don't know. How they made Dale forget he punched me yesterday is curious, too…"

"So, Sal's found a way to reach out from the afterlife. Is it time for a séance of sorts to see if we can find out if he's been talking to Charles Rawlings? Shall we reach out to the otherworldly and dig about?"

I leaned forward and turned the radio to my

favorite preset satellite station. "We definitely should. I don't know if it'll help. I don't know if *anyone* from the other side will help me. All my old contacts still won't show up—probably for fear of retribution, but we can try. I'll tell you this," I said as I pressed a button. "I'm not going to live in fear that every time I go to the mailbox, someone is going to knock me out."

As the music began to play, Win made a face of sheer distaste. "Haven't I asked for forgiveness. Wasn't that enough, Dove? Must you subject me to this cater-wauling?"

I smiled at him. "You owe me after that sideshow at the prison. So, Mr. International Man of Mystery, it's 'I'll Never Break Your Heart' on repeat, and according to GPS, we have an hour and twenty minutes until we reach our destination," I said, my grin widening. Grabbing his hand, I placed it at my heart and sang the chorus as loud as I could. "Sing with me, Win. C'mon. You know the words! *I'll never break your heart. I'll never make you cry!*"

We stopped at the house to grab Whiskey and Bel and headed straight to the shop. I don't know what we were going to stir up upstairs, but we had to try something.

Something was amiss. I felt it in my bones.

As we entered the store, mostly closed for the winter months, I inhaled the scent of sage and lavender smudge sticks and the smell of the hardwood floors, just recently cleaned, as I headed for the beaded back room where our reading table was.

"So the guy acted like he'd never seen you?" Bel asked, his tone perplexed.

I set out the battery-operated candles and put on my Madam Zoltar turban. I always wore it in her honor, whether the séance was mine or someone else's.

Nodding, I said, "Looked right at me and his face was totally blank. But someone's been at him, Bel. I know it. Why would some guy who's never seen me before in his life dress up in a mask and hit me in the face to deliver a message from a dead guy?"

Bel flew to the table and waddled toward me. "So you think that derp Sal didn't cross, and he's been haunting Charles Rawlings in prison? Because I've been thinking about this all day and you've made a lot of enemies, Boss. Some dead. Some still in prison. I'm worried this is bigger than we are."

No kidding. I, too, worried this was bigger than I was. Something I couldn't handle without the backup of my coven. If magic and trickery were involved, I was stewed.

The only witches who would talk to me were Winnie and Hal, if you didn't include my mom and dad, that is. And I wasn't sure I wanted to involve the people I love on the off chance they might end up hurt.

I ran a finger across Bel's soft head. "Let's not think about that yet. Let's try and make contact and see what we can see."

Win sat across from me, voice activating the lights to dim. "Arkady? You with us?"

"Always, Zero," his voice boomed from above.

I bit the inside of my cheek. "Then let's do this." Reaching for Win's strong hand, I gripped it tight and closed my eyes. "Hey, guys? You up there? Anyone? We need a little help."

Nothing. Only the sound of our breathing. "What about you, Sal? Are you up there having a good laugh at my black eye? The one you only wish you could have given to me, but I killed you before you got the chance?"

"Petal!" Arkady hissed with a harsh buzz that echoed in the room. "Do not incite."

"*Bossss,*" Bel whispered in my ear as he sat on my shoulder. "Tread lightly."

But I felt like it was the only thing Sal would respond to. He certainly wasn't going to answer me if I asked nicely and said pretty please with sugar on top.

I squeezed Win's hand, mine a little clammy, just to let him know I had my reasons for provoking Sal.

I lifted my chin and pushed harder. "What's the matter, Sal? Wouldn't the light accept you? Or are you still bouncing around from plane to plane, lost and alone? Poor Sal. You mad?"

Now *Win* looked worried, as the candlelight flickered over the planes of his face. "Stephania..." he said in a low tone, gripping my fingers.

"*Trust,*" I whispered back. Before I said, "Do they make fun of you up there because a girl whooped your behind? Is that why you're sending me messages through Charles and some prison guard? Can't you do it yourself? Or are you too weak to do anything more than whisper sweet nothings in an inmate's ear? Why don't you leave them out of it and come talk to me? Or are you too chicken?"

The table rumbled then, rumbled and shook, but not hard enough to frighten me. Sal—if this *was* Sal— was clearly still too weak to accomplish much but make suggestions to vulnerable people. All the fear I'd had building up all day began to fade.

I chuckled in mock laughter. "Yeah. That's what I thought. You're too big of a wimp to do much. Next time pick a guy who hits harder. Dale was a pussycat compared to some I've fought with—especially you."

When nothing happened, when Arkady didn't intervene with any information, I decided to call it. I was hungry and not nearly as worried as I'd been at the beginning of the day.

Sal had been up to some hijinks, and he might try again, but in comparison to what I'd been up against before, I figured I'd be all right.

"Welp, Sal. It was good talking after all these years. Oh, wait. You didn't talk because you can't unless you use someone to do it for you, can you? Anyway, I'm hungry and tired. So see ya around, douchecanoe."

I was about to rise from my chair when I saw a flicker of a shadow in the corner of the room.

I squinted and looked to Win. "Win, do you hear anyone?"

"No, Dove. There's nothing. Tell me what's happening."

The moment he said the words was the moment an apparition appeared, staticky at first and then clear as day.

I gasped. I gasped so loud, the intake of breath to my lungs hurt.

No. It couldn't be. She'd crossed over. I'll never

forget when she crossed over. My heart had hurt for days afterward.

My fingers gripped the edge of the wood table and I swallowed hard.

"*Malutka*? Talk to Arkady Bagrov. What is happening? You look like you see ghost." And then he laughed at his own joke because, well, I *do* see ghosts, and I was seeing one right now.

But this ghost? It was one I'd thought was long gone. One I was *sure* had crossed over. How was this happening?

Win rose, too, moving to stand near me, keeping me at his side. "Tell me what you see, Dove. Tell me what's happening!"

"Sophia…?" I whispered, swallowing hard, my trembling fingers at my throat where I felt my pulse pound out a beat. "Is that really you?"

Win's head whipped around as he cocked his ear. "Sophia? As in Dana's dead girlfriend?"

"Ye…yes."

She was right in the corner, her dark hair billowing behind her, her beautiful skin incandescent, her hand outstretched.

"Listen, Stevie," she said, her voice hoarse, her tone a clear warning. "Listen to me. *Listen carefully*. Your life depends on this. Do you understand?"

I shook my head in confusion. I didn't understand. I could *hear* ghosts again? I hadn't been able to hear ghosts since what felt like forever. Not since I'd made my own visit to Plane Limbo and we'd taken down those jerks selling body parts at the funeral parlor.

Tears sprang to my eyes. "How…? I thought you'd crossed? How can you be here?" I whispered

"Sophia?" Win called out.

"You can hear her, too?" I asked.

Win looked around the room as though he might actually see her. "Yes…but clearly so can you, Dove."

"*Stevie!*" she hissed my name, her eyes wide and filled with fear. "I can't stay long. The veil is only thin enough for me to push through for mere moments before it disappears. This is why you must listen. *Run, Stevie!* Run as far as you can. He's coming! He's coming for you!"

Her image shimmered and shook, warbled and distorted. "Who? Sal? Is it Sal? *Who's* coming for me?"

She reached out a slender hand to me, her eyes wildly imploring. "Go, Stevie. I'm begging you to go *now!*"

"Where? Where do I go, Sophia?" Panic rose in my voice and my heart crashed, thumping in my chest.

I felt her urgency. I felt it in every cell of my body. It was hot and persistent and filled with the worst fear I'd ever experienced, but I didn't know where I was supposed to go. What was I running from?

Who was I running from?

She shimmered again, the words she spoke becoming unclear and garbled, but I distinctly heard her say "Sal" before she disappeared.

"Did you hear what I heard?" Win asked.

I sighed, pulling off my turban and setting it on the table. "You mean did I hear Sophia say Sal's name?"

Win nodded, his eyes riddled with concern. "Yes. I distinctly heard her say the name Sal."

I gulped. Sophia had managed to find a way through the veil to warn me about Sal. Not an easy task. Not easy at all. Whatever this was about, the afterlife wanted me to know. At least somebody up there still liked me.

Win grabbed me by the shoulders as I thought about seeing Sophia after she'd crossed over. If I had time to consider it, I'd remind myself it was a remarkable feat at the time.

Win looked at me, his face wreathed in his handsome smile. "Dove, you do realize what this means, don't you?"

I shook my head, my brain spinning. "I don't know what any of this means, Win."

He tipped my chin up, forcing me to look at him. "My beloved, you can hear ghosts again. Not just see them, but *hear* them! You haven't been able to do that since the incident in the funeral parlor when you were almost cremated. This is wonderful news!"

I gipped his forearms, my hands trembling. "Is it? Because it sure doesn't feel wonderful. First Dale Rainwater, now Sophia, all warning me about something bad. That somehow isn't my definition of wonderful."

Belfry flew to buzz in front of my face, his tiny yellow snout twitching. "Boss, take a whiff. Take a deep whiff. It's clear as day."

I inhaled deeply, fighting a shudder before I muttered, "Oooo."

"See? ya smell it, don't ya? It's your magic, Boss. I told you!" he sang out, zooming around in happy circles, making Whiskey bark and chase him through the store.

I did smell it this time, and it was a familiar scent as old as time. The scent of my magic, that tangy, lemony odor mixed with sandalwood and herbs.

Each witch has a unique scent, all unto her own, and as much as I wanted to deny it, this time I did smell it.

"Stephania!" Win praised. "I know this frightens you, but it's wonderful news, my Dove."

"Dah, my *malutka*. Is good. So good! I am happy for you."

But I waved it off. I'd been happy before. I wasn't going to let this fool me again. "Look, we don't know if this is just another glitch in the universe, toying with me. It's happened before and then for months, nada."

"But it hasn't happened with your scent. Something big's about to happen, Boss. Something really big!"

The moment Belfry said those words, something big *did* happen. Something a little bigger than even I could anticipate. It was one thing to possibly have my magic return and be able to see and hear ghosts.

Quite another to be shot at.

Yes, folks. Someone took a shot at me.

With a gun.

Directly through Madam Z's glass picture window, shattering it into a million pieces.

As the bullet whizzed past me, I heard Win bellow, "Stephania, duck!" moments before he steamrolled me, covering me with his body and knocking me so hard to the ground I think my bones crunched.

As I lie there stunned and breathless, I heard another shot, and yet another ring out.

"Zero! "Arkady yelled. "Roll under table with my petal now! Do as I say. Take cover! She is coming. You must hide!"

All I could think was *she?* as Win tucked me beneath him and rolled me under the table What *she* wanted to shoot me?

As I heard gunshots ping haphazardly off the walls and various knickknacks, I continued to wonder who she was. I'd tussled with a lot of people, but I'd never tussled with a woman who'd ended up dead. And even if I had—if she was a ghost I'd somehow angered, how the heck had she gotten her hands on a gun? How was she physically *holding* a gun?

Man, the afterlife was sure changing. Ghosts were getting stronger, they were more easily manipulating the vulnerable. The afterlife had gone mad.

My breathing quickened in panic as Win lie on top of me. Thankfully, the tablecloth was long enough to hide us.

I heard whoever it was stomp toward us. "He's coming, Stevie Cartwright! He's coming for you, and Sal says he's going to make your life a living Hell!"

I looked up at Win, his eyes as wide as I'm sure mine were. I recognized that breathy-sweet voice. Was that…*Tammy*? Tammy Parker? The woman who'd slept with her best friend Cleo's husband, Doug, then killed him so he couldn't confess to anyone that he'd impregnated Tammy? And on top of that, killed a witness who'd seen her confronting Doug?

That Tammy Parker?

What in all of cock-a-doodle-doo was going on?

Tammy was in prison. She'd gotten fifty years with no parole for first-degree murder. Unfortunately, during her trial, she'd lost the baby. But how could she be the one shooting at me? I'd testified at her trial, for bleep's sake. I was there. I saw her dragged out of the courtroom, kicking and screaming.

But I forgot all about that when I heard more gunshots. One of my favorite vases crashed to the floor, scattering ceramic pieces all over the surface.

I curled myself into Win, praying someone would hear the shooting and come help. "He's coming, Stevie, and this is your warning!" Tammy screamed, her voice ragged, almost sounding possessed.

"*Malutka*! Tuck in your leg!' Arkady ordered. "She can see your leg!"

She could shoot it, too. Because that's what she did. She shot it.

And phew doggie, it really hurt.

CHAPTER 6

"*P*ut that gun down, you fake-blonde crook!" I heard Bel yell as a searing-hot pain rain through my calf.

Then I heard Tammy's terrified scream and the clatter of something fall to the floor. "Get away from me! What are you?" she called out in hysteria.

"I'm your worst nightmare, blondie!" Belfry yelled.

"She drop weapon, Zero. Get gun! Is by your right hand!"

Win rolled out from under the table and grabbed the gun just as we heard, "Police! Don't move! Put your hands in the air and get on the ground!"

I sighed with relief. Officer Not-as-Cranky-as-He-Used-to-Be was here to save the day.

I saw Tammy fall to the ground and feet rushing toward her before I allowed Win to pull me out from under the table, my leg stinging, leaving a trail of blood.

"You're bleeding, Dove," Win noted as he helped me up and sat me in a chair while the officers on the scene cuffed Tammy, the orange jumpsuit she wore torn and dirty. Win ripped the arm of his shirt to tie around my calf to stop the bleeding, examining my torn skin before he declared it a flesh wound. "She just nicked you, beloved, but we should have a doctor look at it."

As an officer, one I didn't recognize, hauled Tammy upward, she looked at me, her eyes, once bright and blue, now haunted with deep circles under them. Her appearance was nothing like it had been when I'd tangled with her last year. She looked haggard, her roots no longer blonde but a medium shade of brown.

"He's coming! He's coming! Heeee's coooooming for you!" she shrieked with this odd sort of manic glee as she struggled against the officer, her chest puffing outward, her face beet red.

Okay. I'd about had it with the "he's coming for you" baloney on a stick. I wanted answers.

I stomped up to her. Well, sort of. I mean, I did get shot in the leg. So I stomp-hobbled up to her and stuck my face in hers. "*Who's* coming for me, Tammy? *Who?* Sal? Is Sal coming?"

Quite suddenly, she looked me directly in the eye and had the audacity to grin. A grin filled with malice and hatred, but when she answered, her voice was dead and eerie. "You'll see, Stevie Cartwright. You'll see."

"All right, Montrose, get her the heck out of here," Dana ordered before he looked at me, his eyes warm with sympathy even though, as always, his tone was professional. "Miss Cartwright? Shall I call an ambulance? Are you hurt?"

I rolled my eyes at him. "No, Officer Uptight. You should not. It's just a flesh wound according to my spy. I'll be fine with some antiseptic and a bandage. Oh, and a Twinkie. I'm starving. Forget me. Mind explaining how Tammy Parker busted out of the pokey, got her hands on a gun and shot my business up?"

I looked around at the store and the complete mess of shattered glass, scattered herbs and broken windows.

Dana tucked his pad back in the pocket of his uniform. "Mind telling me if you know what she meant by 'he's coming for you'?"

I put my hands on my hips and eyeballed him. "You sure you wanna know what we suspect?"

This would be his first case that had to do with the supernatural since I'd asked him to trust we can communicate with ghosts. In fact, Tammy Parker's case is what had cinched the deal and finally made him believe.

Dana licked his lips and rocked back on his heels. "Does it have to do with spectral beings and the afterlife?"

"It does, bro-friend," Win said, giving him a slap on the back with a chuckle.

He chewed the inside of his cheek, the muscles in his hard jaw working. "Is it something I can legitimately write up in a report?"

Bel buzzed to Dana's shoulder. "Nope. Not unless you want to be the laughingstock of the station."

I crossed my arms over my chest. "Hey, how did you know to come here, anyway? Did someone hear the shots and call you guys?"

"Belfry. He dialed 9-1-1 by voice activating your phone."

I stroked under his ear and blew him a kiss. "You're my favorite bat today, Bel. How very smart of you. Thanks, buddy."

"Indeed, mate," Win complimented Bel. "Well done."

"I think I scared the bleach right out of her blonde hair," he chirped with a giggle. "I buzzed in her ear. Freaked her right out."

Dana pulled out a chair amidst the debris of the broken vases Tammy had shot up, motioning for us to sit. "You okay to answer some questions, ghost lady?"

"I am, scaredy-cat."

His eyes narrowed at me. "I am not scared. I'm just cautious."

Win shook his finger at us, the remnants of his torn shirt, flopping about. "Now, now, children. We agreed to put this all behind us. Dana, you have proof Stephania can see ghosts and is a witch. Stephania, you know Dana has particular beliefs when it comes to his faith. Both of you will be respectful of one another, or I shall have to take drastic measures. Measures neither of you will like. Now, behave like adults, please."

I rolled my eyes, and so did Dana. "Fine. Yes. I'm

okay to answer questions. She only grazed me. It doesn't hurt that much. No, you can't write down why I think Tammy Parker came looking for me because Bel is right. You'd be a laughingstock at the station. So let's keep this simple. Tammy Parker shot at me just after I got a ghostly warning to run."

I had to wonder if Sophia knew Tammy was loose? But I couldn't—*wouldn't*—share that she'd been the one who warned me.

It would hurt Dana, and I didn't ever want to see him hurt like that again. Above all else, he was my friend and he'd loved Sophia deeply. Her death had nearly been the death of *him*. If I could avoid telling him, that's how it would stay.

Dana cupped his chin in his hand, looking more relaxed. "Anything else happen before this? Like, how'd you get that black eye? Do ghosts hit you?"

I smirked at him. "No." I paused a moment and reminded myself that might not be the case anymore, since the afterlife had gone wild. "Well, at least I don't think so. It's been a while since I've been this close to the afterlife, but they can send people to do it for them, and that's what I think happened with Tammy Parker. I think someone from the afterlife got in her ear and helped her break out of prison to send me a message."

Dana shook his head. "She's been all over the news today. I don't know how she did it, but somehow, she broke out of a maximum-security prison, made her way here, got her hands on a gun and came looking for you. It's lunacy. I mean, she was in Smithville, for cripes' sake. That's not an easy prison break by a long shot."

I blew out a breath of pent-up air. "It is if you have help."

Dana eyed me, his handsome face concerned. "You mean ghostly help, don't you?"

"I do."

He threw his hand up in helpless defeat. "How do we fight that, Stevie? What can I possibly do to keep you safe? All I have is a gun and my bare hands. What good is that against a ghost?"

He sounded so helpless. My heart turned over in my chest. I reached over and patted his hand. "You have as much as I do. Maybe more because I don't have a gun, but I'll figure it out, Dana. Don't worry."

He was in friend mode now, and it made me smile. "But I *am* worried, Stevie. A woman broke out of a prison that's almost a hundred miles from here to bring you a message and try to shoot you. What if she'd succeeded?"

Win gave Dana's shoulder a squeeze. "But she didn't, chap. You were here. For the moment, it's quite all right. Let's not dwell on what could have happened."

Then Dana looked at my face, focusing on my eye. "So who gave you the black eye?"

"Mike Tyson. And I showed him who's boss, too. You should see his nose," I joked.

Arkady laughed in my ear while Win snickered.

"Stevie…" he said in his Officer Warning Tone.

I gripped Dana's hand. "I'm not giving up who gave me the black eye because he doesn't deserve to be in trouble for it. He was coerced and used as a pawn by someone in the afterlife, and I won't believe otherwise. So if you promise not to go hunting him down, I'll tell you what happened, extracting names."

"Okay, spit it out before Moore gets here and wants to question you until your eyeballs roll to the back of your head. He was caught up with someone else, so I told him I'd handle this 'til he got here. Hurry up before he does."

Oh, Detective Moore. My least favorite person at Eb Falls Police Department. He was still mad I'd figured out his partner was the one who'd killed Dana's girlfriend (and almost me, too), and it didn't look like he was ever going to get over it at this point.

I told Dana what transpired the night before, leaving out Dale's name and where he worked. But I did tell him the message had likely been first given to Charles Rawlings via Sal Finch, then passed on to someone else.

"So some guy just came up behind you and cracked you in the face? Did you see him as he approached?"

"Nope. Never saw it coming,"

Now Dana's eyes bulged. "Jeez, Stevie, why the heck didn't you call us?"

I made a face of disbelief. "Dana, are you serious? I was going to call you and tell you a ghost sent me a message through some random guy I've never seen before in my life? C'mon, my friend. How would you report that? He specifically said Sal Finch. If I told the police that, they'd laugh me right out of Eb Falls because Sal is dead. Remember him? I was arrested because of him. It wasn't worth the taunting."

He heaved a long sigh. "I don't know how I would have handled it, but I wish you'd tell me who the guy is so I can go find him myself and give him a taste of his own medicine."

I grinned at him, even though it hurt my eye. "Aw, Win. I think he likes me." Then I gripped his hand again. "You can't do that, Dana. You're an officer of the law and a rule follower. People who follow rules don't beat up other people."

I should have known Dana was too smart not to put some of it together. "Wait, isn't Charles Rawlings in Larch for killing your stepfather? Um…what was his name?"

"Bart. His name was Bart, and now I can tell you what I couldn't tell you then. Charles had visions. Bart was a warlock who had an affair with a human. He produced Charles, but never knew about him. Because he didn't know about him, he couldn't teach him how to be a warlock, and his human mother thought he was a psychopath. So she shipped him off to boarding school. And before you say he's a murderer—I know that. But I also know how awful it would have been if I didn't understand my powers and have my mother and my coven to teach me how to use them."

"So who thought it was a good idea to put a warlock in a human prison?" Dana asked, his lips thinning.

"Baba Yaga…remember I told you about her? The witch of all witches? She stripped him of his powers. He's as human as the rest of the prisoners now."

Dana's face proved he understood. "And that's where Sal comes in. He used someone vulnerable to talk whoever the guy was that punched you in the kisser to deliver the message."

"Yep. But here's the clincher. We found the guy, and I swear, Dana, he looked at me like a total stranger. Like he'd never seen me before in his life. It was, at best, creepy."

Dana sucked in his cheeks, the wheels in his head turning. "First of all, you were all over the papers when that bit with Bart went down. I'm surprised you weren't on *Dateline*. So I'm doubting he didn't recognize you. In fact, you've been in the papers more than some celebrities these last few years for all the crimes you've solved. Second, Larch is max security. Only approved visitors. That means the person who attacked you had to be someone who visited him or someone who works there, am I right?"

I entwined my fingers and shook my head at him. "Dana…" I said with a warning tone. "I'm begging you not to get involved with this part of things. Not with Charles, anyway. You're dealing with the supernatural. It's not like a human investigation. The person who slugged me doesn't know who I am, or his memory of me has been erased. Let it be. I mean it. Or I'll put a hex on you that'll make you breakout with a severe case of backne. You got it? This person doesn't remember hitting me, and both Win and I believe him. Period. An innocent man shouldn't go to jail for assault and battery he was coaxed into by something and someone he couldn't see."

"She's right, mate. I was as angry as you that she'd been hit, but there's no way he could have faked his reaction to her," Win backed me up.

"Okay, so let's go back to the evidence. He said the same thing as Tammy. Sal's coming for you. How can he come for you, Stevie? He's dead."

"As was I, mate. Surely you recall that," Win reminded him.

Dana gripped the edges of the table. "Let me process. The reincarnation thing still gives me the chills. No matter how long we're friends, that's always going to be the case, Win."

Win held up his hands and grinned. "You'll get no argument from me. I, too, get chills."

"I've said it a hundred times, it's not an easy process, Dana," I reminded him. "It takes a will of iron. It's as rare as hen's teeth. But it has happened."

"But you were determined to get to Stevie," he almost whispered, his voice low and hushed as he looked to Win.

My throat tightened up. He was thinking of Sophia and, I'm sure, wondering why she hadn't tried the same —making me doubly certain I shouldn't tell him the ghost who'd warned me about running was Sophia.

I rose and hugged him hard around the neck, knowing he was thinking of his lost love. "Win's struggle was long and painful. Some ghosts don't even know about reincarnation, Dana—or they wouldn't even consider it because of their faith. You know what that's like, right?"

He knew I understood his thoughts, and showed me by giving me a hard squeeze back, his answer so sad, I felt it in every crevice of my heart "I do know."

"So how would you like us to explain this to Detective Moore?" Win asked, changing the subject. "Shall we simply tell him Tammy Parker came gunning for my fiancée because Stephania proved she was a murderer and ruined her wedding and play it off as though she's barmy?"

Dana nodded and smiled. "Let's go with barmy. You're both right. I can't explain it all to anyone, but I'm going to find out how she got out of Smithfield. I know you say she had some ghostly help, and I'm sure you're right, but maybe I can find out something else that will help."

Just then, Detective Moore stomped in, his feet traipsing to the back of the store with reluctance in every step.

Dana gave me another hug and whispered, "Please be careful, Stevie. I don't know how to help, but I'll do whatever it takes to keep you safe."

I gave him a quick kiss on the cheek and promised to be careful before he left, and I turned to face Detective Moore, as sullen and pouty as ever, his black trench coat covered with a fine mist of rain.

I smiled at him. "Well, look who it is. Starsky without Hutch. How ya been, old friend?"

He grimaced at me as he pulled out a pad. "Always with the jokes," he snarled. "Let's get this show on the road, Miss Cartwright."

CHAPTER 7

"Honestly, even when I'm the one being shot at, even when I'm the victim, Detective Moore always manages to make me feel like I'm the guilty party."

Win laughed as he shook the wok with our stir fry, the scent of chicken and green peppers making my mouth water. We were busy preparing dinner and talking over the day's events when he reminded me, "I hate to break this to you, Dove, but you do antagonize him. The comments about Hutch don't help."

I put out our plates and napkins on the table in the breakfast nook and rolled my eyes. "You're right. I do antagonize him, but he's been holding a grudge since Ward Montgomery tried to kill me. He behaves as though I took his playmate away—not take a murderer out."

Win brought the steaming wok to the table and smiled at me as he set it on a trivet and placed a

69

chopped pomegranate for Bel in a small bowl. "Two wrongs and all those fancy metaphors, beloved."

I poured us some white wine and settled into my chair, only to hear Arkady back him up. "Zero is right, cornbread. You must let go. You never know when you might need his help."

I snorted, putting my napkin in my lap. "It'll be a cold day downstairs before I need his help."

As Win dished out my serving, his eyebrow rose. "Some could say the same for Arkady and I. We were once sworn enemies, and look at us now. Chums 'til the end."

"I am at the end," Arkady said with a laugh. "Now I must wait for you all over again. But I keep seat on bench warm for you all. Someday we will be together and have party."

Win tipped his glass of wine upward at his friend in salute. "Cheers."

"I can't think about a time when I might need Detective Moore, but who knows. Stranger things have happened."

"Either way, dig in, Dove. You've had a long, hard day. You need nourishment."

I jabbed my fork into a piece of chicken—chicken Win always managed to keep tender and juicy while crispy—and popped it in my mouth, chewing thoughtfully.

"Do we really think Sal, that total wimp of a man, is trying to reincarnate himself, or is he just finding someone gullible, vulnerable enough to do his dirty work to try and scare me? He didn't seem like the type of guy who was capable of seeing past the nose on his face. Everyone keeps yelling he's coming for me, but I think it's more like he's just trying to intimidate me."

"He did die mad as a hornet, Boss," Bel said. "If he wanted revenge, it's not like it would shock me if he did everything in his power to reincarnate."

I was so angry, I could spit. That weakling was somehow trying to figure out how to get back to this plane? Who knew a sissy like him could be so motivated.

However… "How am I supposed to fight off the supernatural—alone? If he does reincarnate and he gets here and he comes for me, he might have powers I can't defend myself from. So how do I protect us?"

Bel sat back, his round belly full of pomegranate. "With your magic, Boss."

Magic-schmagic.

"And me," a familiar voice said.

My head whipped around to find Hal, my sister, standing behind me. I jumped up and gave her a hug, loving the scent of sugar cookies and cinnamon in her hair. "Hal! What are you doing here?"

She gave me a hard hug and set me from her. "You don't really think this man who loves you more than the Earth would let you do this alone, do you? Do you think I would? Not on your life, big sister."

Win rose and grabbed another plate. "You didn't think I'd allow you to be defenseless, did you, Dove? I've put in a call to Winnie, too."

I twirled a piece of Hal's shiny hair around my finger and grinned. "Where's Hobbs?" He was her new boyfriend, a super-sweet, Southern guy we all really liked.

"He's using our time apart to catch up on some work," she said with a wink and a coy grin. "We've been getting to know each other and it's sort of consumed us. We've kind of ignored the outside world a little. But he said if you or I need him, all we have to do is call."

"How's your grandmother and Atticus…Stephen King?" Stephen King was her boyfriend's rescue bull-dog. Another reason I loved Hobbs—he loved animals the way we all did.

Halliday and I talked often over Zoom since we'd found each other and when we did, it was as though I'd known her forever. "How about the new kitten and Phil? They getting along?" I asked, avoiding the reason Hal had come.

"Everyone's great, Stevie. All healthy and happy. But we're not here to talk about me. Let's talk about what's happening with you."

My heart began to pound in my chest with worry. "But what about Baba? Aren't you afraid she'll take drastic measures and punish you for mingling with me?"

Hal shrugged and tucked her blue sweater around her. "What *about* her? Listen, Baba can say whatever she wants, do whatever she wants, but I'll be danged if I'm going to let someone hurt you when you're without your powers, Stevie. It's like putting an infant in the middle of a highway to fend for themselves. My loose circle of witch contacts would never allow it. So, Baba can suck my tailpipe if she doesn't like it, and I'll tell her so myself."

I felt such a wave of relief wash through me, it almost knocked me over. "Thank you for coming, Hal. You have no idea what it means."

"It means we're going to figure this out. So let's get the show on the road." Hal rubbed her hands together in delight when Win set the plate before her after taking a deep whiff. "Chicken stir fry, I love it! So tell me everything and I'll tell you what I know."

I cocked my head at her. "What *you* know?"

Her gorgeous blue eyes searched mine, her shiny black hair gleaming under the light fixture above. "I had a vision, Stevie. I'll explain after you give me all the details."

As we ate our meal, and I told her what had occurred thus far, she sipped her wine and nodded quietly.

I took my last bite of chicken, wiped my mouth and said, "So that's my story. What's yours?"

Her shoulders lifted as she sighed, and it wasn't a good sigh. It was heavy and filled with dread. "Now, you both know how my visions work, right? I don't know what tense they happen in. Past, present, future, yes?"

I did know that. I also knew her spells gave her trouble more often than not when she was stressed, but her visions were usually spot on—even if they didn't always make sense at the time.

I nodded, bracing myself. "Right."

"About ten seconds before Win called, I was having lunch with Hobbs and all of a sudden, I'm in some snowy forest. It's freezing cold, my lips are so cold I can hardly move them, but it doesn't matter, because as you know, I can't talk during a vision."

I took a big gulp of some more wine. "Uh-huh."

She grabbed my hand and held it tight. "Now, listen closely to me, Stevie. My visions don't always happen exactly as I see them, okay? Sometimes they're simply metaphors for what could happen if I don't stop it or what's already happened. When I finish telling you, it'll be obvious this hasn't happened."

I inhaled and blew a breath out as Bel climbed on my shoulder and Win held my other hand in his grip. I felt Arkady's warmth surround me as Hal continued.

"So I'm in this forest, it's frigid and you're on the ground," she said softly, her voice trembling ever so slightly. "And a very large man is standing over you in a hospital gown. I got the impression he was sort of old school; you know? Like, 'Hey, little lady, shouldn't you be in the kitchen making me a sandwich?' I don't know why, but it was just the vibe I got from him."

Gripping Win's hand, I had a bad, bad feeling I knew who she meant. "Did you get his name?"

"That's part of the weirdness of this whole vision. I saw a hospital chart with his name, Hank Endicott. Sound familiar?"

"More than familiar. He's the man I told you had an affair with his son's husband. He had a heart attack the night we fought each other. But he's in jail with no chance of parole for killing his son's husband."

Hal made a face of distaste. "Oh, yes. I remember his story well."

"So he was the guy standing over me?" I almost squeaked the question.

"Yes. And just as I got a really good look at him, a cell phone appeared out of nowhere and he answered it and then he looked down at you and said, 'We told you he was coming for you. You were warned.'"

I licked my lips, my heart thrashing against my ribs. Taking one more gulp of my wine, I asked ever so tentatively, "Was I dead?"

There was a deep silence for a moment—one where Hal looked to Win and then Belfry. She was afraid to tell me, but I was a big girl and I refused to live in fear.

"It's okay. You can tell me, Hal."

A tear slipped down her rosy cheek. "You were a husk of a shell. It was your soul, Stevie. Whoever left you lying in the snow took your *soul*."

And as witches, we both knew what that meant. If I lost my soul, I would turn to nothing. There'd be no levels of planes or lights calling me home.

Everything would simply cease, and I would fall into a hole of nothingness.

CHAPTER 8

I held up a finger and said, "Can you guys just gimme a sec? I need some fresh air."

Win moved to rise and follow, obviously to attempt to console me. "Stephania…my Dove—"

But I really didn't want to sob like a baby in front of everyone. "Just give me a minute, would you, please?"

I heard Arkady tell him to let me gather myself and I heard Hal's chair scrape as she got up to console Win, but I needed a second to gather myself here.

"Um, no. You're not going outside or even to the bathroom alone after what I just told you," Hal said. "I'll give you your privacy, but I'm sticking close."

I waved a dismissive hand at her, but I didn't try and stop her because she was right.

Pulling open the French doors, I took a step outside and deeply breathed the cold night air. I'm not ashamed to admit, at that moment, terror crept into my bones, the fear so deep and so raw, I doubled over and tears stung my eyes, not just from the cold, but from fear.

How did Sal, of all people, have this kind of power over me? For that matter, how did he have this much power over the afterlife? What was I going to do to keep myself alive? Worse, why were all my past dealings with criminals coming back to haunt me now? How had he managed to get through to the people I'd put in jail?

I'd been out of real touch with the entities I used to communicate with on the reg for far too long. The afterlife was changing, and because I only had a one way-ticket to upstairs, and most of my old contacts were too afraid of Adam Westfield and his power, I somehow think I was missing a bigger piece of this puzzle.

Strike sat in his heated house and as I approached, looking for a little love and sympathy, he didn't shrink away from me this time, but he continued his hesitant behavior.

"It's okay, buddy. I get it and I love you anyway," I said before I turned and looked out at the water. Dark and choppy, it rolled along as the raw wind blew, bending the barren trees in the backyard. The whistle of the breeze rang in my ears, the sound lonely and empty.

I've been afraid before, but tonight? Tonight, I was terrified, not as much for myself but for all the people Sal was involving. Dale, Hal, Win and Bel.

"Stevie?" Hall called, coming up behind me and gripping my shoulders.

I scrunched my eyes shut and fought a shiver. "Thanks for coming, Hal. I'm so grateful for you."

She hugged me tighter. "You'd do the same. Have you tried to reach Dad or your mother?"

I shook my head. "I haven't, but last I knew, Dad was in some remote part of Borneo doing a movie and unreachable, and my mother's in Africa—somewhere. I don't have the kind of witch power to reach them and calling them hasn't worked out."

She pulled me tight to her chest from behind. "But I do. I can find Dad, for sure."

But I patted her hand and shook my head again. "No, don't do that yet. Please. I don't want to upset them until I have to."

She spun me around by my shoulders and looked me square in the eyes. "You don't think if you end up kaput, the idea they could have helped will upset them less?"

I smiled slightly. "No. I just mean that together they're like siblings, fighting like I'm the last piece of pie at Thanksgiving. They both think they're the one who's right and I can't take the arguing now. But I won't hesitate if things get worse."

"Promise?" she asked, her deep blue eyes closely watching mine.

"Promise," I said firmly.

"Question?" Hal asked.

"Of course."

"How much worse does it get than someone trying to shoot you?"

Chuckling, my breath came out in a puffy cloud. "I meant if it continues. Maybe Sal's done the best he can and his juice has run out? You know it takes a lot for a ghost to perform earthly acts. Maybe he's exhausted his arsenal and this is over."

Hooking her arm through mine, she directed me toward the house. "I confess, I don't know a lot about ghosts, but you know what I do know about?"

"What?"

As we stepped back inside into the warmth of the house, she said, "Magic, and I can smell it on you, Stevie. Bel's right. Something's happening, and I'm going to help you figure out how to manage it."

"As will I," said a British voice, as deep and sultry as Lou Rawls, seconds before he appeared.

"Atticus?" I said in disbelief. There was no mistaking that voice.

I loved Hal's hummingbird familiar. He was funny and smart...and most of all, he had magic just like Hal.

He buzzed toward me in all his tiny green and red glory, and pecked my cheek. "Indeed. 'Tis I, young lady, and together, Hal and I shall refresh your memory about your magic so we might fight this battle once and for all. I won't have anyone haunting our own."

"Ah, my good man, it's wonderful to see you," Win said with a smile. "Always good to be with another Brit."

Win and Atticus went off to chat all things British

and Bel took Whiskey, who still felt the same way about me that Strike did, while Hal snapped her fingers and did the dishes.

All while my heart glowed with the love I was lucky enough to be surrounded by.

"I smell it, too, Stephania. Your Belfry is right. Your magic is coming back. Now try again. Just one more time. I know it's been a taxing morning but since when has a witch ever given up?"

Atticus buzzed around my head and settled on the buffet in the front entryway, where we had a beautiful fake arrangement of flowers and the bowl for our keys —the buffet I'd been trying to make disappear for two solid hours now.

It was a gorgeous piece Win had found a few months ago, a deep mahogany antique he'd had professionally refinished to a lighter oak with crossbar doors and heavy black handles on the drawers.

Every time I'd make at least a part of the table vanish, like a leg or a drawer, it would come right back, only bigger—almost comically so.

Win was going to kill me when he saw we had a buffet that looked like a lopsided woodworking nightmare.

Yet, I continued to concentrate as hard as I could. Making things disappear was a huge part of being a witch.

If you were in a sticky situation, all you had to do was snap your fingers and voila, you were gone. That sure would help when being chased by some guy with a gun, right? I've lost count of how many times that would have helped me.

Except, I wasn't doing such a great job of making anything but my self-confidence disappear.

And still there was so much more to relearn. This wasn't even the tip of the iceberg.

Hal, dressed in worn jeans and a pink thermal shirt, nudged me. "Listen, don't be discouraged. When I'm stressed and scared, I suck at spells. Ask, the outer reaches of Siberia, because I've been there," she said with a laugh.

"And don't forget the Stay-Puft Marshmallow Man you made appear on your last adventure," Atticus reminded her.

"But I got the job done, didn't I, you little wanker? I solved the bloody crime, now didn't I?" Hal said, mimicking his British accent, making us all giggle.

I laughed at the image of the Stay-Puft Marshmallow Man from *Ghostbusters*, helping to solve a crime.

Hal squeezed my hand. "Listen, all I'm saying is, we're not perfect. I'm far from perfect, but your magic is there and it's ready for you to use if you can just harness it."

I appreciated the vote of confidence, but this morning had exhausted me. I needed a break from the hope she was instilling in me.

As if on cue, Win came down the stairs and said, "Why don't we break for a bit? I've made some clam chowder in honor of our guests from Maine, and I'll make a pear and hazelnut salad with warm walnut-apple dressing for lunch. Then we can all take a breath and regroup. Yes?"

My shoulders sagged, but my heart lifted. Win always knew what I needed—even if he didn't think it was a hot dog. "Can I have a Twinkie afterward?"

"Bah!" Atticus chided. "Food for heathens!"

Win chuckled as he sauntered into the kitchen with Atticus buzzing beside his head. "If I've said that once, I've said it a thousand times. My beloved eats like a first grader."

They both laughed as they made their way to the kitchen when the doorbell rang.

"I'll grab it," I called, looking up at the video screen to see who it was.

Someone with a big bouquet of flowers. I peered closer to see it was Edmund, who'd once worked with Petula, from the bakery. He'd left after the death of the famous Chef Le June, who'd died after eating a poisonous cake at my Christmas party.

Edmund had also been possessed by Adam Westfield, and as a result, had kidnapped Belfry under the influence of Adam's dirty magic.

Thankfully, he didn't remember being possessed, nor did he really understand why he needed a change of scenery—thus working for the florist—and why that change of scenery was helping, and I was glad for that.

I was glad he didn't remember *anything* he'd seen or heard that horrible night.

I popped the door open and smiled at him, admiring the beautiful bouquet of pale pink peonies mingled with baby's breath and white hydrangeas.

I thought how strange it was to be able to find peonies and hydrangeas at this time of year, but what did I know about how a florist went about getting their stock? I bet they were from Win. He loved having fresh flowers in the house, but he loved sending them to me, too. Sometimes just to tell me he loved me or he'd been thinking of me.

Maybe he'd done it to cheer me up?

"Hi, Edmund! Long time no see. How've you been?"

He smiled at me, but it felt a little vague and unsure, and really, who could blame him? He'd been possessed by a warlock who wanted to kill me, and I felt sure some of the fear he must have experienced, even if it only felt like a dream, still lie beneath the surface—somewhere deep inside his brain.

"I'm doing well, thank you," he responded, his rain jacket wet from the walk up the drive, his face mostly hidden by the hood on his coat. "These are for you." He shoved the bouquet at me and turned to leave.

But I stopped him. "If you wait just a second, Edmund, I'll grab you a tip."

But he continued anyway, calling over his shoulder, "No thank you, Miss Cartwright!" before he ran back down the steps and jumped into his small Prius and took off.

Okay, weird. Who doesn't want a tip? Especially from me. I'm a big tipper.

Win came up behind me and rubbed my shoulders. "Lunch is getting cold, Mini-Spy."

"*Someone* sent me flowers," I said, my tone flirty and teasing.

"How lovely. Who are they from?"

I shrugged, confused. "I thought they were from you—you know, to cheer me up."

"Nay, Dove. As much as I wish I'd thought of the idea, knowing how much you love hydrangeas, 'twas not I. I opted to make you a Twinkie cake and buy you a case of grape Fanta whilst you spent the morning toiling with your magic."

I pulled the card from the plastic stick that held it in place just as I heard Win say, "Ticking. I hear ticking."

I cocked my ear and listened. "Yeah, me, too. What the heck—"

I didn't get to finish. Win grabbed the basket of flowers from me so fast, he almost knocked me over. "Back away, Stephania! Get back!" he yelled before he ran out into the pouring rain and launched the basket as far from the house as he could, throwing it like an NFL quarterback.

The second he let it fly from his hands, it roared to life, blowing up in a huge ball of fire, sending flowers and debris everywhere, landing as far away as the edge of the cliff at the end of our lawn.

Everyone came running to the door as I stood there

shivering. Hal wrapped a sweater around me, but nothing could warm me up.

Someone had just tried to blow me to smithereens.

How rude.

$\mathcal{I}$ stood by the fire in the living room, trembling. As I read the card out loud again, I shivered. *"I owe you one! Love, S."*

Hal snatched the card from me and crumpled it up. *"Now* will you let me call Dad? This is getting out of hand, Stevie. This nutso wants you dead. He just tried to blow you up. I don't know how he's doing it, I don't know as much about the afterlife as you, but whatever's happening here is dangerous. Dad's a powerful warlock. He can help us. Whoever this Sal is, he almost killed you!"

"But he didn't..." I know, I know. That was a weak response at best, but it was true. He hadn't succeeded. That was all that mattered for now.

Hal planted her hands on her slender hips. "What if he had? What if that were pieces of *you* all over your lawn, Stevie? If Win hadn't heard the ticking of the bomb—a *bomb,* dear sister—you'd be like a jigsaw puzzle all over your lawn—one I'm pretty dang sure I couldn't put back together. Enough of this already. I'm getting in touch with Dad. We need all the warlock/witch power we can get."

She stomped off to the kitchen and we followed. I sat down at the kitchen table, stunned. Absolutely stunned. Sal really wanted me dead. Sal had actually found a way to reach this plane and the people in it and he was using them to get to me.

I mean, I got it, don't get me wrong. I did take what was supposed to be his and then sort of killed him. But I didn't kill him on purpose, and I sure didn't mean to take Win's riches.

"We need to call florist, my pierogi, and find out who pay for flowers," Arkady said. "We need clues."

"We need to call the bomb squad," Hal said dryly, her eyes narrowing.

Win kissed the top of my head, now dry and changed, as was par for the course. He looked no worse for the wear. "Trust that I've handled the bomb with Arkady's help. We've defused many bombs in our time, haven't we, old chum?"

"Do you remember time in Macedonia, when we save Duchess of Salisbury from blowing up in the lady's room in her mansion?" Arkady asked.

Win nodded and smiled, as if he hadn't just defused a bomb. "I do, old friend. We were working toward the same cause on that case. Good times, eh, comrade?"

"Gentleman!" Atticus reprimanded. "'Tis not the time for a stroll down memory lane. Might I remind you, someone just tried to blow up your fiancée, sir. Certainly, we must act and act now!"

Hal was in the process of grabbing her puffy vest and pulling her hair up into a ponytail. "I say we start at the florist's. They must have some record of who paid for them. And maybe Edmund remembers something about the delivery."

My heart was still throbbing painfully in my chest, but she was right. I was going to go to the florist's and poke around. Adele Perkins owned Flower Power, her shop, and she was an acquaintance—she did all of our floral arrangements for parties and such, and she was part of the garden club. Maybe she'd help a girl out.

I went toward the door to grab my coat, but Win lightly gripped my arm.

"Stephania, it worries me, you being out in the open. Look at what happened in the safety of Madam Zoltar's. Look at what happened in our own home, for bloody sake."

I looked up at him and cupped his cheek, smiling warmly. "So you expect me to stay here and wait for something else to happen? Is that what we do when there's a mystery to solve, Spy Guy? Or do we seize the tiger by the tail and figure out what's going on?"

He gave me his, "Cut it out, Stephania" look. "The mystery doesn't usually involve you—or at least not this closely. I'm worried, Stephania. I wish you'd lay low and let us do the rest."

I looked up at the ceiling as if Sal could hear me—I hoped he could. "And let some weenie try and have me killed because he's too chicken to do it himself? I don't think so, 007."

Win knew there was no arguing with me. He knew when I sank my teeth into something, I wouldn't let go until the end. Even if it meant *my* end.

His lips went thin, but he didn't disagree. "Then wait and I shall get my coat. The two of you aren't going without me."

Hal smiled at me as Win left the room to get his jacket. "He's only being overprotective because he's crazy about you, and you know it. He fought long and hard to get to you. He's never going to let you stray very far when there's danger in the foreground, Stevie." Then she looked around the kitchen as if she were seeing it for the first time. "It's beautiful in here. So warm and comfortable and not at all pretentious. Did you have a hand in decorating this? You've done an amazing job."

Now I laughed. "Um, no. This was almost all Win. He can do it all, cook, decorate, reincarnate, defuse bombs. I eat Twinkies and almost get myself killed. He'll be thrilled to hear my ex-interior designer sister approves."

"He is, indeed, thrilled. Upon our return, I have a few questions about a room upstairs. Might I pick your brain later this eve, Hal?" Win asked with a smile.

"Absolutely. All right. Let's go see a florist about a bomb," Hal said, clapping her hands together, her lips a grim line.

"Worry not about dinner. I shall prepare it," Atticus

called after us. "Hal? You know what to do if you need me."

She gave him the thumbs up and blew him a kiss. "Thanks, Atti."

As we made our way out to my car, Whiskey ran behind me, with Bel yelling to him. "Get back here, you big beast! You're going to get all dirty again. Argh, you're like herding cats!"

I turned to send Whiskey back inside, but he surprised me when he came up to my hip and nudged it in the familiar way he always did when I was going somewhere, driving his enormous head into my hand and licking my palm.

Tears sprang to my eyes and I took a deep breath. Maybe he was coming to like the "magical" Stevie? "I love you, too, bud."

I scratched his ears, which appeared to satisfy him, and he turned and ran back inside, leaving me feeling a whole lot more like everything might be okay.

As I got in the passenger seat, prepared to find out who'd sent those flowers, I thanked the universe for Whiskey's small gesture.

***

"Hi, Adele!" I called out as we entered the shop, filled with cases of beautiful roses and various floral arrangements on doily-covered tables.

Vases in all array of colors stood on shelves, and

little stained-glass butterflies in a bowl, made by a local artist, were by the cash register.

Cheerful and bright, with colorful flowers every-where, the shop was a nice respite from the gloom of the day.

Adele turned with a smile, but when she realized it was me, her smile dimmed a bit. Even when she looked at Win, whom she adored, her eyes held suspicion.

Wiping her hands on her apron, she set down a pair of shears at her workspace and approached us tenta-tively. "Hi, Stevie. What can I do for you?"

The vibe I was getting was all-out bizarre. Adele was one of the friendliest people I knew. Outgoing and fun, she was in her mid-fifties, but looked forty at best.

She worked out and jogged, and we'd often see her on the pier in the summers, getting her steps in. She always waved and smiled cheerfully at us, never anything but warm and welcoming.

I decided to try again. Reaching for her hand, I smiled and said, "It's so good to see you, Adele. How was your holiday? Busy, I imagine?"

But she shrank back a little from me before she briefly touched my hand then took a step away, her nostrils flaring. "It was good."

Hal decided to take over, and thank goodness, because I was currently at a loss. Sticking her hand out, her face beaming, she said, "I'm Halliday Valentine from Maine. I'm here visiting Stevie. Lovely to meet you."

Adele, a little less tentative now, replied, "Hello.

Good to meet you, too." She paused for a moment and gave Hal the once over. "So you're from Maine, you say? It's pretty cold there this time of year."

Hal chuckled and rocked back on her feet. "If you only knew. Your weather here in Ebenezer Falls feels like spring compared to where I come from."

Adele set the shears down and nodded. "I'll bet. So how can I help you?"

Maybe start by telling me why I've become public enemy number one in my own hometown?

Hal stepped in front of me and hooked her arm through Adele's as if they were old chums. "Stevie got the most gorgeous floral arrangement from you today, and I was wondering if I couldn't have one made and sent to a friend. I loved it so much, I'd like an exact duplicate."

At first, Adele looked confused again. "I don't remember anyone ordering an arrangement for Stevie," she said as though we were speaking in tongues.

Hal pulled the crumpled card from her jacket. "This card is from your shop, isn't it?"

Adele took the card in her slender fingers and nodded, still looking quite confused. "It is...but I don't...I don't remember making an arrangement for Stevie."

"That was me," said a lanky girl with chestnut-colored hair in one of those cute messy buns I could never manage to achieve on the top of her head.

As she approached, she didn't appear at all afraid of us as she wiped her wet hands on her red apron. I guess she didn't get the memo that I was the town pariah today.

I noted her nametag read Brenda as she looked me directly in the eye. "Hydrangeas and peonies, right?" she asked, all business.

I nodded, finally finding my voice. "That's right. But I don't know who this person who sent it is. It was signed only S. I was wondering if you could tell me so I can thank them because they were so beautiful."

She wrinkled her nose. "It was a call-in. They gave me a credit card number, but asked to remain anonymous. Maybe someone's got a crush on you?" she teased. "Bet your handsome man here isn't too crazy about that."

If wanting me dead is the new crush, then yeah, Sal had a crush.

"So it was a man who called the order in?"

She smiled, young and pretty, her skin glowing, and winked. "It was, and that's all I can tell you."

Adele, still standing there looking utterly lost, looked to Brenda. "Why didn't you tell me there was an order for Stevie?"

Now Brenda looked at *her* with confusion. "Since when do I tell you when there's a new order? I do it all the time, Adele. I answer the phone and take the info and the order, and then I make it and arrange delivery."

Brenda said it to Adele in a rather "duh" sort of tone. As if to say, when did that become a problem?

"You're sure it was a man who called in the order?" Hal asked as Win put his hand at my waist.

Brenda cocked her head and grinned. "What makes you say it was a man?"

Hal drove her hands into her jean pockets. "Because you said it might make Stevie's fiancé jealous."

"That doesn't mean it was a man. It could have been a woman," Brenda said, now sounding a little annoyed. "Listen, I have a bunch of orders to fill. I can't tell you anything else. Is it all right if I go do my work now, Adele?"

Adele seemed to snap out of it. "Of course, Brenda. Thank you."

Just then my phone pinged with a text. I pulled it from my purse and saw it was from Hal.

Stevie, keep Brenda busy with how beautiful the arrangement was. Win, you get Adele in the back to show you some flowers or something. You're in the garden club together, and you could charm the pants off the Pope—get her away from the register with a question about garden club. And I'll look at those orders by the cash register. I'll text you when I'm done.

Got it, we both answered.

I strolled over to Brenda's work station, littered with green stems. "Hey, Brenda, mind if I ask you a question while you work?"

"You bet," she replied with her beaming smile, busy putting together some yellow roses and ferns.

"Those hydrangeas, where did you get them this time of year? And for that matter, the peonies? They were beautiful. I didn't know you could get them so early in the year."

Win approached Adele by putting his hand at the small of her back and steering her toward the back of the room. "Adele, quick question. Do you remember chatting at garden club about the Black Lady's Slipper orchid? I'm absolutely fascinated and considering one for myself. Do you still have it in the greenhouse?"

Now she smiled as though she suddenly remembered who Win was. "I do. Would you like to see it?"

"As much as I'd like to see Elvis rise again," he teased, and she giggled like a schoolgirl.

Ten minutes later, Hal texted us both and we made a swift exist from Adele's store.

As we stood outside the flower shop, I leaned back against the brick façade. Taking in large gulps of breath.

"What was that about? Adele looked at us as though we'd killed kittens."

Hal grabbed my hand and pulled me toward Strange Brew. "Let's grab a coffee and I'll explain. C'mon, Win, our girl needs a boost of caffeine."

We strolled across the street toward the coffee shop, me still in a weird daze of confusion and a disoriented state.

Win pushed open the door, holding it for us as we entered our familiar coffee shop. Forrest was still off somewhere in the world on sabbatical, but Chester was ever present, as was the manager we'd become acquainted with.

The scent of mocha and hazelnut wafted to my nose, soothing my frazzled nerves.

"There's my girl," Chester called out as he dropped the newspaper and rose to greet me. He came over and gave me a peck on the cheek. "Still as pretty as ever, and still with the man who talks funny, I see," he teased Win.

"It isn't easy to keep her from you, good man. As handsome as you are, you've given me a real run for my money, you cheeky devil, but I'm doin`g my best," Win joked back, shaking his hand.

Chester ran his thumbs under his suspenders and eyed Hal with a wide grin. "And who's this looker?"

Hooking my arm through hers, I grinned at him. "This is the sister I was telling you about, you Mr. Flirty McFlirt. Halliday Valentine, meet Chester Sherwood. One of my favorite people in Eb Falls."

Chest grinned at her, his pudgy cheeks lifting upward. "Well, helloo there! Heard lotsa nice things about you from my girl here. You here for a visit?"

"I am. And some coffee. I hear you have the best in town."

Chester put his hand to his chest. "You sure know a way to a man's heart. C'mon. Let's get you all some." He tugged her off to the counter while Win and I found seats.

I sagged against the back of the wrought iron chair, looking down at my fingers in my lap. "Well, at least Chester still likes me."

Win reached for my hand and kissed the tips of my fingers. "Adele still likes you, Dove. Something's amuck. We'll find out what this is about. Until then, please try and remain as calm as possible. I know that's the worst thing to say. It sounds so condescending, but it's necessary if we hope to get to the bottom of this. And we will."

He was right. I squeezed his hand and gave him a weak smile just as Hal showed up with three steaming mugs of coffee, a cookie hanging out of her mouth, and took a seat opposite us.

I blew on my double mocha before I asked, "So what did you find out?"

She leaned into us, her face somber. "First, the weirdness with Adele? Someone's been in her ear. She doesn't understand it, which explains her confused, almost frightened look when she saw you, Stevie. So whoever got to her must've told her to be leery of you. It won't last long, but for now, she's afraid and doesn't know why."

"She's always so friendly," I admitted. "It was so strange. My feelings are really starting to get hurt here."

Hal nodded as she took a bite of one of the freshly made cookies Strange Brew sold. "She's under some kind of spell. I could smell it all over her. I don't know who did it, or how, but it was obviously to keep her from knowing about the bomb, or even the flowers, for that matter."

"Yeah, the bomb. I wondered about that. But Brenda didn't say anything unusual—not that she'd admit to putting a bomb in my flowers. But if she didn't, who put it in there? Edmund? Someone who told Edmund to do it? And where the heck did he get it?"

Hal leaned forward and whispered, "I don't know, but there doesn't seem much that's impossible for the afterlife. Now, last but not least, before we go any further, tell me something."

"Sure," I replied, a bead of sweat breaking out on my forehead. "Anything."

She fingered the napkin, brushing crumbs from it. "Who's Egan Joseph?"

Win and I looked at each other in complete shock.

"Why do you ask, Hal?" Win queried, running his fingers over his squared jaw.

Hal looked at us hesitantly. "Because he's the one who sent the flowers."

So, way back when Win was first getting on his feet and I was sucked up into the afterlife, there was an incident with a guy from a morgue.

That meant, the guy from the morgue who'd been selling body parts and had received hardly any prison time at all for doing so—even though he was in cahoots with The Vera Brothers Funeral Home, who he sold the body parts to—and was now under house arrest, had sent me flowers with a bomb in them?

That Egan Joseph?

CHAPTER 10

"You're kidding me? How did you forget to tell me you've been to the afterlife, Stevie?" Hal asked from the back of the car as we drove toward Seattle to find Egan Joseph.

Hal had used a locating spell after looking at his all-but-abandoned Facebook page, where there were plenty of comments about what he'd done from random people, but nothing from him. And now we were on our way to try and talk to him.

Sighing, I shook my head. "So many things have happened since I met Win, I forget sometimes."

Hal reached forward and poked my shoulder. "Stevie? Leaving this plane isn't something you forget. Dying and trying to find your body so you can get back into it isn't something you forget."

I rolled my eyes. "I guess because it was such a scary, yet awe-inspiring time, because I met Arkady but was almost cremated, I try and block some things out.

But mostly it's because that creeper Egan was selling body parts to funeral homes, Hal. It was awful. *He* was awful."

She squeezed my shoulder from behind. "I bet it was, and I'm sorry you went through that. Still, that you neglected to tell me you've been to the other side is pretty forgetful, and when this is done and we're sitting around by the fire with a bottle of Napa Valley Cabernet Sauvignon, from the awesome year 2017, you can tell me all about it. I want to hear every detail."

"Oh, magnificent year, Hal. Well done," Win praised her as he hopped on the highway.

Laughing, I had to agree. "That's fair. Regardless, who coaxed Egan Joseph, who's on house arrest for the next year, to call in and send me flowers, and who put the bomb in them? He sure didn't construct a bomb himself. He can't leave his house to buy supplies. I mean, there's always online shopping, but I'd bet he's monitored pretty closely if he has Internet at all."

Win gripped the steering wheel with force, his knuckles whitening. "I still can't believe he wasn't punished more severely. Two years then released with time off for good behavior and a house arrest? He sold pieces of people. *People*, Stephania. The American justice system enrages me sometimes."

"It enrages us all sometimes. But here we are," I said, rubbing his upper arm. "Regardless, the Vera brothers and their mother are still in prison. So there's hope for us yet. Nonetheless, I get the feeling Egan's going to have the same story everyone else has. That he has no idea how or why he called in an arrangement and had it sent to me. I'd bet an organ on it."

"Stop betting body parts, young lady," Hal warned with a shaky chuckle.

As we pulled up to an old, worn apartment building made out of fading and cracked gray brick, across the street from an abandoned parking lot with a torn chain-link fence and garbage blowing in the wind, I shivered.

Win ran his knuckled along my cheek. "Dove? Are you all right? Shall you stay here with Hal and I'll go speak with him?"

I popped the passenger door open. "Nope. This is my doing. Because of me and my snooping, we're all in danger. I'll do the talking."

"You do know that's not true, especially where Egan Joseph is concerned. Surely, you do, Dove."

But I'd forgotten the circumstances under which we'd met, and as we headed toward the rusty elevator and hit the number of the floor his mailbox said he lived on, I wasn't thinking of much beyond how I would likely get the same message I'd gotten from everyone else.

I owe you one.

As we stepped out of the elevator, Win set me behind him, and under normal circumstances I'd have something to say about it. I'm not a radical feminist. I don't mind a door being opened for me, or a man rising when I leave the table, but I absolutely can take care of myself.

Yet today, I had my doubts. I was fighting unseen forces. That said, I let him rap on the red, chipped door with his knuckles. Obviously, Egan would be home.

The sound from the TV was loud, but he must have heard the door because he popped it open, poking a bloodshot eye out of the chained latch.

"Yeah?" he asked, his wide face and rotund body the same as when we'd last seen him.

Win put his hand on the door and eyed Egan. "Mr. Joseph? Do you remember me?"

Instantly, he had a look of terror on his face, his bloodshot eyes wide. "Aw, no man. No way! I remember you and that fancy accent. You go away. I have nothing to say to you! You're evil!"

I couldn't resist sticking my nose in. I stood on tiptoe and talked over Win's shoulder. "We just want to talk, Egan," I soothed.

His face went pale white when he saw me. "I don't even know how you're talking now, you lunatic! You were *dead*. Deader'n a doornail when I took you out of that car!"

"You mean, *stole* my car," I reminded in a dry tone…

If you'll remember, Egan, being the entrepreneur he was at the time, had decided to find bodies for the Vera brothers all on his own. He took my body to the morgue and brought my car to a chop shop.

"Well, obviously I'm not dead, Egan. I'm standing right here in front of you." I twirled around and smiled. "See?"

"Go away!" he roared, sweat beading his pockmarked brow, sheer panic in his tone. "I don't want nothin' to do with whatever's going on here. Leave me alone or I'm callin' the cops!"

I'm not sure what happened to me then. I was angry and frightened and he'd done something awful—something he probably didn't even realize he'd done, but he could have blown me to pieces.

Though, to be honest, he had sold body parts for cash and paid a very small price for doing so. He almost deserved what he got next.

Pushing Win out of the way, I put my hand on the door and said, "All we want to do is talk to you for a minute, Egan. Please, open the door!" I hissed.

Let's just say, the door opened. In fact, it *blew* open. Ripped right off the hinges and flew across the room, sailing right into the window by the fire escape, making it explode outward in shards of glass.

My mouth fell open and I looked to Hal, sending her a signal with my eyes to ask if she'd done it, but she silently shook her head no.

I'd done that?

Cheese and rice.

Regardless, I behaved as though I had every confidence in the world when I sauntered into Egan's smelly apartment, the scent of TV dinners and sweat most prominent.

With both Hal and Win's mouths open in shock, I grabbed the door and hauled it toward the entrance. I placed it against the chipped wall, patting it with my hand.

"There," I said with a smile at Egan. "All better. Now, we have some questions for you. Please, sit." I pointed to the worn green velour couch.

He shrank back from me, his tracking bracelet securely around his ankle, the red dot glowing in his drab apartment.

Speaking of drab, there were cracks in the ceiling and the tiny kitchen with its scarred Formica countertop and beat-up avocado refrigerator had crooked cabinets with missing doors.

There wasn't much to the place, but what there was depressed me.

Egan shuffled across the worn-thin shag carpet. "Look what you did to my door! Are you crackers?"

I took a seat on an old tan recliner, crackled with wear and reeking of cigarettes. "Probably, but I need some answers. And speaking of crackers, wasn't it you who was going to sell my body parts and my car? I'm not sure how you define crackers, but I'm pretty sure you win first prize."

His face went passive, but I still saw his terror, clear as day. "What do you people want? What could you possibly want to talk to me about?" he asked with a trembling voice, dropping onto the couch.

He looked a mess in his wife-beater sleeveless shirt, stained with something yellow, and a pair of ratty black sweats with holes and paint splattered on them that had seen better days.

"What do you Satan-worshipping people want?!"

"If we're throwing around names, I prefer Beelzebub, but if Satan's the word you want to use, far be it from me to stop you."

He'd called me a devil worshipper because he was sure I'd risen from the dead. Which, technically, I had. But that didn't make me a devil worshipper.

Everyone always called witches devil worshippers. It was so unoriginal.

Oh, how misguided humans could be.

Win began to speak, but I held up my hand to show him I had this. Yet, he still placed his hands on my shoulders from behind to let me know he was there.

"Why did you send me flowers, Egan?"

He gave me a look like I'd lost all my marbles. "Flowers? I'd send Hell flowers before I'd send you flowers, and that's sayin' somethin'."

"Forgive me for my disbelief, but again, wasn't it you who sold body parts for cash? Did I mention the flowers had a bomb in them?" I asked, tucking my purse under my hands.

His face screwed up, even if he still sat as far away as he possibly could from me. "I'm tellin' you, lady, I didn't send you any flowers. You're not gonna blame me for somethin' like that. If my parole officer got wind of it, he'd send me straight back to that hole of a disgusting prison. For the record, I'd just as soon jump off the roof of this building than send you flowers for what you did to me. You ruined my life!"

Before I could say anything else, Hal pulled a piece of paper from her pocket and held it up under Egan's nose. "Do you have a credit card, Mr. Joseph?"

He snorted as he looked around and spread his flabby arms wide. "Does it look like I have a credit card? I live in this dump. After your friend ruined my life, I had to move here because I couldn't afford anything but government-subsidized housing."

I wanted to taunt him with the fact that it hadn't been me breaking the law by handing out arms and legs like Halloween candy. I'd hardly been the one to ruin his life, but I kept my big yap shut so as not to exacerbate the situation.

Hal's lips went thin. "Mr. Joseph, I have zero time for your nonsense. I suggest you try the truth here."

"Or you'll what?" he sneered, clearly trying to maintain his dignity, but then his eyes went wide. "Hey, are you one of these nuts, too?"

Hal's sigh was ragged. "It's rude to call someone a nut, Mr. Joseph. I'm not a nut, but I can be very dangerous in ways you'll never understand. Now, do you want me to call the company and find out if this number is your credit card? Or are you going to show me the card?"

With a scoff, Egan stubbornly shook his head almost-bald head, still attempting to puff his chest out and maintain his manhood. "I told you, I don't have a credit card, lady."

Hal, obviously not in the mood for his nonsense, used two fingers and her magic to gesture at Egan, making him rise from the couch on stiff, quite obviously unwilling legs.

She put her hands on her hips as though daring him

to disobey her. "Go get the credit card, Mr. Joseph. Get it now. I want to compare the numbers."

Egan moved with rigid movement and skirted the couch, backing away to go through a door, which I assumed led to his bedroom. He came back with his wallet and handed it to Hal, his eyes shifty.

Hal dug through the moth-eaten leather and pulled out a couple of pictures and his credit card.

"Are you unfamiliar with what a credit card looks like, Mr. Joseph? 'Cause this sure looks like one to me." She compared the paper and the card. "Now let me have your email and password so I can log into your account."

Egan gave it to her with no trouble, his voice wooden and flat, and then Hal handed the card back to him.

The moment he touched the card was the moment everything changed. The room grew warm, almost unbearably so, and Egan's face went red, his body unyielding.

And then those all too familiar words. *"He's coming for you, Stevie! He owes you one!"*

I was up in an instant, approaching him, my eyes narrowed and filled with anger as I waved a finger under his nose. "Who had you send those flowers, Egan? Who got the delivery boy to put a bomb in them?"

Quite suddenly, everything about him changed. His attitude, his stance, the look on his face. He went all slouchy and relaxed, his face went smug and when he spoke, it was as though a light switch had been flipped.

"The delivery boy didn't do it. I made the bomb. It was easy-peasy-lemon squeezy. I just looked it up on the Internet."

That took me aback. I looked up at his oily skin, shiny with perspiration. "How could you get a bomb to the delivery boy? You can't even leave the house?"

"Shucks," he crowed with an eerie grin. "You must not think too bloody much of me if you think I couldn't accomplish such a simple task. I had him come here first and I dropped it in there. I mean, duh. It wasn't that hard."

Okay, he was scaring the life out of me. I'll never forget the sound of Sal's voice, his accent, so much like Win's…and Egan sounded exactly like Sal Finch.

Not to mention, he was bragging. When we'd busted open the door, he'd been terrified. Now he was boasting his accomplishments. His entire demeanor had changed as he plopped back on the couch and looked up at us with a cocky grin.

"*Who are you?*" Hal seethed, sniffing the air. "By the power of the goddesses near and far, I compel you to show your true face!" She whispered something in Latin I didn't quite hear and snapped her fingers.

He cocked his head and smiled again, letting his ankle with the bracelet rest on his opposite leg. "Huh?"

"Is he under some kind of spell?" Win asked, coming to stand near me.

Hal nodded her glossy black head, pushing me

behind her. I felt her hand tremble as she gripped my arm. "Something's so wrong here, Stevie. Something worse than evil."

I clenched her arm, suddenly feeling more afraid than I'd ever felt before. "He...he sounds just like Sal. I'll never forget what he sounded like," I mumbled. "Let's go, Hal. *Let's go now.*"

"Let's go, Hal," he mimicked me, grinning at me with a wink. "You'd better listen to her, Hallie-Oop, before you get hurt."

In a sudden fit of rage and frustration, I screamed in his face, "Why are you doing this, Sal? What do you want from me? You want another round? I'm not afraid of you. So, c'mon, let's do it!"

He jumped up from the couch as though he was ready for a knock down drag out, but then Win intervened.

"Stephania!" Win called, but I was so angry I shrugged him off.

Yet, as quickly as it began was as fast as it was over. Egan shrank away from me again, walking backward until the backs of his knees hit the sofa and he fell back down on it. "I want you to get the heck out of my apartment and leave me alone! That's what I want. I don't know what you're talking about. I didn't send you any flowers, especially with a dang bomb!"

Hal eyeballed him again, up and down, searching his face. "He really doesn't remember anything."

"Then let's go. *Please,*" I urged, grabbing Win's hand and pulling him toward where the door used to be.

Hal followed behind us, making a circle with her finger and reattaching the door.

We all got in the elevator in silence, each of us clearly lost in our own thoughts.

And my terror.

I was lost in my terror.

Because somehow, Sal had managed to possess Egan. Even if only for a moment.

Was possession suddenly the new black?

We wandered into the house, all of us exhausted, but the smell of something delicious made it easier to let go of the fear of the unknown from this afternoon and welcomed me like a warm hug.

Atticus flew into the hallway and Whiskey bounded in behind him with Bel on his back. "Welcome home, Stephania. How went the day?"

"It's more like how didn't the day go?" Hal said to him, holding out her hand so he could land in her palm. She kissed him on top of his head. "It was long and we didn't really get anywhere or learn anything, but we did break a door."

"With your magic, pet?" Atticus asked.

Hal shook her head and grinned. "No, with my big sister's."

I threw up my hands. "I didn't mean to do it. I don't even know how it happened. I just wanted to get inside

Egan's house and *kablam*, it blew the door off the hinges."

"And it was magnificent, Dove. You should have seen her, mate," Win praised.

Atticus flew directly toward my face and virtually squealed his delight. "It was your emotions, Stephania! You were angry, and with good reason. They played a role in breaking the door down. While destructive, and definitely in need of curbing, this is wonderful news!"

I couldn't acknowledge what I'd done right now. I still couldn't believe I'd done it. I didn't even feel it. Used to be, I felt the magic coursing through my veins. But everything was out of whack, and maybe this particular type of magic—whatever it was—was out of whack, too.

"Let's talk about it later, okay?" I dropped my purse on the smooth marble counter of the island and inhaled whatever Atticus was preparing. "Thank you so much for making dinner, Atticus. It's been a brutal day."

Atticus shooed us toward the kitchen nook table. "Off with you then. Sit down, all of you. The wine has been chilled and poured and the cassoulet should be out of the oven at any moment. Do rest your weary feet whilst I finish up the bread."

We all trudged to the table and plopped tiredly into chairs. Whiskey approached me and dropped his head in my lap. I'm not sure if that meant I no longer smelled funny to him and my magic was gone, or if he was simply adjusting to my new scent. Regardless, I kissed the top of his head and scratched his velvety ears, grateful.

Bel hopped up on my shoulder and snuggled against my ear. "See, Boss? I told ya he'd come around. Now tell ol' Belfry what happened today."

As we talked about what we'd learned at Flower Power and Egan Joseph's, Belfry chastised us.

He hopped off my shoulder and onto the table. "You ninnies went to the house of the guy who sold body parts? Have you lost your marbles? He's dangerous!"

"And he's under house arrest and I'm a witch," Hal reassured Belfry as she stroked the top of his head. "It was fine, Bel. I'd never let anyone hurt Win or Stevie. Besides, Egan Joseph was harmless with his ankle bracelet and dirty shirt and sweats. He's pretty defeated."

Atticus flew to the table and waved a wing, producing a large blue cast-iron pot and a basket with two loaves of sourdough bread, alongside a bowl of whipped butter. "My beautiful girl knows her stuff. It simply gets mixed up from time to time and we have blunders, but we always land on our feet, don't we, dumpling?"

Belfry buzzed up into the air to face Atticus. "Don't get your beak in a twist, I'm just saying that guy was a real freak, and he did some freaky things to *my* beautiful girl. I'm not a fan of her having visitation with a guy who sold body parts from his job at the morgue for Happy Meal money."

"Whatever is a Happy Meal?" Atticus quipped.

"Boys!" I scolded, rubbing my temples. "We're both fine and we didn't learn much, other than Sal apparently has learned how, even if only momentarily, to possess a body."

That shut both of them up.

Win began serving everyone as Atticus hopped on my shoulder. "My apologies, Stephania. I didn't know."

I pecked him on his tiny beak, putting my napkin in my lap. "It's fine, Atti. We're all fine. Now while we eat, tell us what you know about possession."

He flapped his wings. "I know 'tis possible. Crispin…er, Christoph has proven that."

Hal chewed on a piece of bread, slathered in honey butter. "But I thought it was rare, as rare as hen's teeth. Yet I'm telling you, Atti, that guy Egan changed. One minute he was terrified of us, and with good reason. Stevie blew his door apart and broke his window. But out of nowhere, he's talking with a British accent and, according to Stevie and Win, he sounded just like the bad guy from the first crime Stevie ever solved."

Atti snorted in disdain. "You mean the one with the same last name as mine?"

I cocked my head upward to look at Atticus. "You remember his last name was Finch?"

"I do, and it makes my wings curl," he spat. "So you're telling me, this man Sal, your first crime solved, is dead, and today you saw him possess this Egan Joseph? What is the afterlife coming to?"

Nodding my head, I shivered. "He sounded exactly like Sal."

Win, too, nodded his head. "I can confirm he sounded just like my twit of a cousin, who, if you're wondering, left this Earth irate because I left everything I owned to Stephania."

Atti sat quietly for a moment before he repeated, "Possession, eh?"

Hal nodded. "That's what I'm asking you, Atti. I thought possession and reincarnation were rare, but look at Nana Karen and Win."

Nana Karen was Hal's grandmother. She'd reincarnated as a reindeer and lived in Hal's barn, where she was happy as a clam. It's a long story, but suffice it to say, reincarnation exists.

And it feels as though it exists a lot more these days.

Hal set her fork down and took a sip of her wine. "All I know is, I smelled evil today, Atti. Pure, unadulterated evil, and it was rancid and scary. We might need to break out the big book of spells and rid ourselves of this monkey on Stevie's back. Call it out —whatever."

Win, who'd been quietly eating his cassoulet, finally said, "There's a book of spells, did you say?"

Atticus bounced his tiny red and green head. "Oh, indeed. It's ancient, but I can summon it, if need be. There must be a way to rid ourselves of this pest!"

Atticus suggesting the book of spells gave me chills. I hadn't seen it in years now. Not since I'd left Texas.

Hal agreed. "Atti's right, we need to call on the book and maybe do an incantation or a summoning."

Win looked rather pale at this point, and he'd

stopped eating altogether. "And what exactly does this involve, Hal?"

Hal shrugged, looking down at her bowl. "A cauldron, bat hairs, maybe some mandrake root."

I giggled when Belfry said, "It does not. Hal's teasing you. It involves summoning the spirit world and asking questions of the spirits."

"But didn't we just do that when we had the séance, Dove?" Win asked, looking a bit relieved.

I nodded. "We did, but some spells call on different types of spirits. I can't do that because I don't have witch powers anymore, but Hal can."

"Correction," Belfry reminded, his voice cheerful. "You have *some* witch powers, Stevie."

I wrinkled my nose at him. "Well, it's not enough to summon the parts of the afterlife we *need* to summon to get some answers."

"But it will be, and it'll be just like old times, Boss. Just you wait and see."

It had been a long time since I'd summoned specific spirits from the afterlife. A very long time, and the thought almost made me tingle. But just a little. My hopes had been dashed far too many times, and like I've said. I don't know if being a witch is even what I want anymore.

It comes with a host of complications I don't know if I'm prepared to handle. When I was a witch, I was a single witch. It's different when you're in a relationship where the footing changes drastically.

Atticus flew to the middle of the table. "Then do

finish your meals and we shall clean up and begin. We'll find out if this punk who shares my name is behind this and banish him for good!"

Hal began to laugh so hard, tears rolled down her face. "*Punk*, Atticus? Since when have you ever used the word punk?"

"Since I became quite trendy and began watching *MTV*. Now hush, child, and eat your dinner. You'll need your strength.

I smiled in appreciation at Atti. "Atticus, I can't thank you enough for coming. Both you and Hal. I don't understand what this is or why it's happening, but your expertise is greatly appreciated."

He flapped a dismissive wing. "Bah! You'd do the same for Hal. How many times have you talked her through a crime? Talked her off a ledge? Given her advice over a Zoom call? More times than I care to count. Now eat up, lovely girl. We have an albatross to remove from your neck."

As I finished up the delicious cassoulet and I thought about seeing the book after all this time, a book once available to all white witches, I felt a sense of calm wash over me.

I don't know why. I didn't even know if it meant anything other than I felt safe with Hal and Atticus here, but I was ready for whatever was coming next.

I think.

"Must it be so dark when we do this, Dove?" Win asked as he stood, holding my hand in the circle of bodies we'd made in the dining room with the three of us.

"It won't be for long," I whispered back. "Are you afraid because it's spoooky?"

It did look a little like a scene out of some witch movie.

Win straightened his shoulders and gave me that haughty look he was so good at. "Afraid is the wrong word, Stephania. Tense is a better adjective. Call it irrational, but I sometimes wonder how I actually made it here, and I oft think someone might want to force me to go back to Plane Limbo. As though I've broken some afterlife rule. When we commune with the spirits, it's almost as though I'm waving a big red flag and they'll find me as a result. Now, from my understanding, these are different spirits. Unlike the ones who seek our help. Yet, still...I find my hesitance is quite real."

Huh. I'd never thought of it that way, but I understood it. Squeezing his hand, I said, "That makes so much sense it scares me. You don't have to stay, Win. You could lay low in the guesthouse, if you'd rather."

He kissed the tip of my nose. "And leave you here alone with a spirit that might cause you harm? Not if the skin were peeled from my very body under the hot July sun as someone poured vinegar over my open wounds."

Hal leaned into him with a chuckle and knocked his

shoulder with hers. "Okay, lover boy, that was graphic. We get it. You have Stevie's back. Let's get back to the business at hand, please?"

Win cleared his throat. "Of course. Just tell me what you need me to do and I'm all yours."

My palms began to sweat as I looked around the dining room, a room we only used when we had large gatherings that included Dana, Chester, Enzo, Carmella, Sandwich and the like. We'd spent many holidays together, birthday celebrations, a dinner for my engagement to Win. So many happy times had occurred here.

It was a beautiful room, with silky curtains that billowed to the floor in a creamy white and the rectangular table in a dark wood with comfortable chairs in a cream linen all around.

I particularly loved the candles on the table. In varying heights, they sat in rustic white candleholders that had once been finials, with a bread bowl in the middle filled with faux cactus.

I prayed, whatever we summoned, didn't make a mess in here.

Refocusing, I watched Hal snap her fingers and the candles came to life, leaving a soft glow all about the room, making it look even more like a movie set than ever.

Atticus sat in the middle of the book with Belfry by his side, in the center of our circle. "Are we ready, chap?" he asked.

Belfry nodded, his tiny face serious and solemn. "Let's contact some ghosties."

They both rose in the air and the book flipped open. Then Atticus began to chant, "Oh, great book of spells, we seek a reply. Who calls upon this plane with great malice and anger? Who hunts one of our own? We need an answer!"

I waited, holding my breath and clinging to Win and Hal's hands, my heart crashing in my chest, my legs like wet noodles.

What if we actually did get Sal here and he was stronger than Hal and Atti? Then what?

When nothing happened, Atti repeated the words, ratcheting up my already heightened fears. "Oh, great book of spells, we seek a reply. Who calls upon this plane with great malice and anger? Who hunts one of our own? We need an answer!"

It became so quiet; you could hear a pin drop. In fact, I think I heard my hair growing, it was so soundless. The room became almost oppressive, as though someone were squeezing the life out of it—like we were in some kind of vise grip.

And then the floodgates opened—and they opened wide.

A warm wind from nowhere whipped the curtains around, making the flames of the candles bounce and flicker. The chairs at the table scraped at the wood floor as though someone were pushing them in and out from the table.

A low hum of noise grew and grew until it was no longer a hum, but words, voices, calling all at once.

The voices mingled and meshed together, and I could only decipher a few sentences. "Stevie! Why are you here? Stevie's back! Stevie, it's not safe! Where have you been! I can't find my brother! Stevie! Stevie! Stevie!"

I looked to Hal, Atti and Bel, who all gave me blank stares...but Win knew. Win heard them, too. I knew because he looked at me with eyes filled with wonder.

The level of intensity amongst the voices grew, becoming impatient for answers until I yelled, "Hey! I'm happy to see you, too, but knock it off, guys! I'm only one person. That means, I can only hear one person at a time. Now shush and settle down. *Please.*"

With that, the room went silent again.

And that was when everyone I think I've ever helped, talked to, crossed over, heard their tale of woe, helped find a missing item, contact a loved one, appeared.

Everyone.

Did I say everyone?

ell, I mean it. Everyone. Even some ghosts from my teenage years were there, all smiling at me.

"My *malutka,* what have you done?" Arkady asked, awe and wonder in his voice.

I put my hands on my hips as I looked at all the faces crammed into the dining room, almost all of whom I recognized from one point in my life or another.

"Well," I said with a wince. "Summoned the afterlife? *All* of the afterlife."

"Okay, Stevie, what's going on?" Hal asked, her face a mask of concern in the candlelight. "I don't see or hear anything."

Atti buzzed toward the ceiling, shooting upward like a rocket. "That's because you can't see or hear ghosts, my sweet pet, but Stevie...Stevie can! Oh, Stevie, don't you see what's happening here?"

I slouched a little, grabbing the back of one of the chairs to steady myself. "I'm not sure, Atti. What *is* happening here? Because I see a lot of entities, and I do mean a lot. All entities I've helped at one time or another, all staring at me."

"Stephania, surely you understand," Atti reprimanded with a sputter of laughter. "You now can see *and* hear ghosts again! You'd lost that ability for several years but it's coming back, and they've come to help. They answered your call!"

Um…huh.

I scratched my head. "But didn't we call on the bad entity who wants me dead? All these souls don't want me dead, do they? Because if that's the case, this is gonna be a bigger ghostbust than I've ever done. We might need help."

Atti flew into my eyesight. "We called for *help*, Stephania. We asked for an answer from the afterlife, and they've come to help, despite their fear of retribution from this Sal."

"We've missed you, Stevie," a man called from the back of the room.

"It's so good to see you again, Stevie! We've heard rumors about how you were over the years, but it's so wonderful to know you're well," a cultured voice I remembered said. "You look stupendous and, above all, happy."

I looked into the crowd of faces and, sure enough, it was Professor Tim, one of my all-time favorite ghosts.

Man, did we have some chats, me and Professor Tim. All throughout my early twenties.

"Professor Tim?"

He wavered in and out like static on a TV, but he nodded his half bald, bespectacled head. "Yes! Oh, Stevie, I'm so glad you're safe. I thought about you every day while you were gone, and if you remember, ghost time feels so much longer than real time."

My smile wavered as I fought tears. This was really happening. I was really seeing and hearing ghosts again. Nodding, I said, "I do remember, and I've thought about you, too."

"Who's your handsome fella?" Professor Tim asked with a wink. "Is he the legend who possessed a real body?"

Win looked around the room, and I pointed him in the direction of the bay of windows. "He is. International Man of Mystery, meet Professor Tim. Tim, meet my fiancée, Crispin Alistair Winterbottom. Tim died in 2004. We've been friends a long time."

He held his hands up to his heart. "How thoughtful that you remember when I left this Earth, Stevie. One of my favorite things about you was your attention to detail. I've missed our chats. I hope we'll have more soon, now that you can see and hear me again. I hope I can chat with your handsome beau, too. We're all fascinated by his possession."

My heart virtually glowed. "Me, too, Professor Tim. I'm so happy to see you, I could burst." I wished more than anything I could hug him.

Win smiled. "I can't see you, sir, but it's a pleasure to meet you just the same."

Professor Tim, a creative writing teacher, died of lung cancer in 2004, and he'd reached out to me to make sure I got a number to a student for a publishing friend of his, who Tim thought could turn his student into a fiction-writing superstar.

And he had. He was off selling books like mad now, and knowing I'd helped, even just a little, made my heart happy.

Then I frowned. "You still haven't crossed? I thought by now you surely would have chosen to go into the light."

He brushed his hands over the front of his argyle vest and smiled. "I'm on a plane where there are more books that there are stars in the sky. I don't know if I'll ever be ready to leave."

Tears sprang to my eyes. "Ah, your love of reading. You taught me to love the classics." Then someone else caught my eye. "Lottie? Is that you?" A woman in a torn parlor maid's outfit from 1812, she'd died in a carriage accident. Her hair, piled atop her head, mussed and wet on one side, and her white cap still askew and dirty, made me smile.

Lottie was a feisty one if I remembered right. She'd refused to cross over because she liked the freedom roaming the planes allowed her—a freedom not afforded her in all the days of her life, days spent answering doors and serving the family she'd worked for.

She shook her finger at me, but there was a twinkle in her eye. "It is, you naughty girl, deserting us like that. How could you?"

Then in the crowd, I saw Finster Lork and Donnie Max. Jimmy-Don Lester and Vania Vitatelli. So many familiar faces, I didn't know what to say.

Tears streamed down my face. "How are you all here? *Why* are you all here? How did those of you who've crossed break through the veil? What's happening in the afterlife?"

There was grumbling and discontent and then someone yelled, "It's fallen apart without you, Stevie. All sorts of out-of-whack things are happening. We need your help!"

I sighed a grating release of breath, my throat tight as I caught sight of Langford Russell in his familiar overalls and flannel shirt, a famer back in the day. He'd died of natural causes and had contacted me to ensure his horse would go to a good home. He was rough around the edges, but kind and a fellow animal lover.

"But you all know I can't help you. My powers are gone. I didn't desert you, my powers deserted *me*! You know what happened. I don't even know how you're here, let alone how to help you. I'm the one who needs help. There's someone trying to kill me. His name is Sal Finch. Do you know him?"

The moment I said Sal's name, and I do mean the moment I said it, the room began to quake and the wind picked up again, a wind so strong, it blew us up against the walls.

Pandemonium ensued and then every entity in the room began yelling at once. "Stay away from him, Stevie! Run! Fight him! Fight for your life!"

They all began to fade in and out, flickering and shimmering as though they were going to leave.

My heart began to hammer in my chest. "No!" I yelled. "Don't leave. Please! Come back so we can talk some more! I've missed you all so much!"

In that moment, in that very moment, I realized I *did* miss this aspect of being a witch. Professor Tim had shown me that. We used to have lengthy conversations about so many different things. I'd learned so much from him, and now, who knew if I'd ever see him again.

Seeing them all was like showing me a life-size Twinkie I was only allowed to look at, not eat.

But they were gone. The room settled back down, the curtains fell back into position and the candles stopped flickering.

Everything felt...deflated.

My shoulders slumped as Win wrapped his arms around me and hugged me to his chest without saying a word.

Hal put her hand on my shoulder and squeezed. "They'll come back, Stevie. You're only getting stronger. I don't know how you're doing it, but I'm pretty sure it's because you're amazing. So Baba Yaga can stuff it in her stupid leg warmers. You're going to get your powers back. I can feel it."

If you'll all recall, Baba loved the '80s and dressed as

though Madonna was still the Queen of Pop and leg warmers and ripped sweatshirts were in vogue.

Taking a deep breath, I decided enough was enough. No more whining in fear and cowering because of stupid Sal Finch. I decided to instead bask in the gratitude for the chance to feel the connection to the afterlife again—even if it might only be this once.

Kissing Win's cheek, I gave Hal's hand a pat and straightened my shoulders. "Okay, enough is enough. It's time to figure out what's happening here and what Sal wants. We didn't get any answers."

Bel nuzzled my ear. "But you did get a lot of love, Boss. That was nice, wasn't it?"

I smiled, my chest tight. "It was, and now, let's open a bottle of wine and solve this mystery the way we do all the rest."

"Will there be cake with that wine, Atti?" Hal asked with a chuckle.

I grinned as I made my way back to the kitchen where Whiskey and Strike snuggled on the floor in Whiskey's orthopedic bed. "There'll be whatever you want if you help me solve this mystery."

"Of course, pet. Whatever your heart desires."

"Chocolate?" she asked hopefully.

"Is there anything else?" Atti spread his wings and a three-layered chocolate cake with fluffy whipped chocolate frosting appeared on the table.

Win got the glasses for the wine and we all sat down.

There was no laptop we could pop open to look at

Facebook pages, or Twitter feeds to scroll. There were no pictures of a crime scene to examine. None of the usual tools we used were available this time around.

Just some heads put together and good old-fashioned crime solving.

I hoped that would be enough.

I yawned and stretched my arms, looking at the clock on the stove to see it was almost one in the morning. The faces around the table told me it was time to call it a night.

There wasn't much more we could do, anyway. Atti had another call out to find a particular spell, a stronger one, to help us rouse Sal and push him to show himself, but we hadn't heard anything back from his contact yet and we'd mostly come up dry with much in the way of clues.

There were no clues like there were when we were solving a real-life mystery. There wasn't really anyone to talk to because no one remembered anything that had passed between them and Sal.

Though, Hal had looked up Egan Joseph's credit card statement online and it showed he placed the order the day before I got the flowers.

We still needed to speak with Edmund, but I already knew he'd have no memory of who told him to put a bomb in them. Sal made sure of that.

"You know what I keep thinking, my sweet sponge cake?"

I rubbed my grainy eyes. "What's that, Arkady?"

"Does this Sal only want to see you in pain? What is end game? Does he really want you dead? Or only to toy with you? He keep saying he owes you. That is message every time, but what happen when he is tired of cat and mouse?"

I leaned forward on the heel of my hand and yawned. "I have no idea. He probably wants to possess a body and come for me. For sure, he wants me dead. I mean, I did steal all of Win's riches from him."

Win grabbed my hand and kissed the tips of my fingers. "You didn't, Dove. I willingly gave them to you, knowing they'd be better handled with you."

I pressed the back of his hand to my cheek. "I know. What I mean is, he feels like I stole it all from him, and there was a lot to steal. Then I killed him."

Bel clucked his tongue. "You didn't really do that either, Boss. He fell."

"All of that's true, but maybe he's been simmering all this time, angry because he thinks I stole his life, and he's been exploring ways to get back to this plane and get rid of me."

Hal pulled the tie from her ponytail and shook her glossy black hair out, running her fingers through it. "But how could he get his hands on Win's riches? There'd have to be a will of some kind naming him as the beneficiary, right? Something that said all this belongs to him. And I'm pretty sure you guys had a new will drawn up, didn't you, Win? So even if Stevie dies, the money would go to you. And if you both die, it can't include the next of kin because technically, you have no next of kin as Christoph? So what could Sal gain other than the satisfaction of seeing Stevie kaput?"

Win nodded, finishing his last sip of wine. "Yes. We had a new will drawn up in the event we both take a nosedive. Some money goes to various animal and children's charities, but the house and all its contents and the remaining money goes to you. As well as Belfry, if you'll have him."

Hal gasped and blinked her beautiful blue eyes. "Me? Oh, Win. I couldn't...I mean, of course Belfry, and Whiskey and Strike, will always have a home with me, but I..."

Win's smile was soft. "You can and you will, and you'll use it in good health. Come here in the summers and enjoy the amazing weather we have. This house was built with love and care. That needs to stay in the family. You mean so much to Stephania, you've given her a connection she didn't know she had. It's had great meaning to her. That had to be acknowledged. Please don't turn that down. Besides, we made sure the will was ironclad. Sal couldn't get his hands on anything even if he hired the best attorney this side of the Pacific Northwest."

Hal looked down at her fists and rubbed them against her eyes. "I..." Then she inhaled. "I won't turn it down, but there'll be no more talk of death and you guys not being here for the moment. I won't have it. I refuse—"

Hal stopped speaking, sitting upright in her chair, her spine erect, her eyes focused forward.

"A vision?" I asked Atticus with a wince.

"Yes, poppet. Let the moment pass. I promise it shall. Until then, simply remain nearby on the off chance she needs support."

Scooting my chair closer to Hal's, I stroked her hair as Win held her hand and Belfry snuggled on her shoulder, and we waited in silence. I knew what to expect when this happened to her. You just had to wait it out while she sat like a statue until the vision released her.

Two minutes or so later, she slumped forward with a jolt, her face pale.

I took her hand in mine. "I'm here, Hal. It's all fine. You're in my kitchen, everyone's here and all is well."

Suddenly, she twisted in her chair and looked at me, her eyes clearer now and filled with a fire I hadn't seen before. "Talk to me about tacos."

Tacos? I could sit all day and talk about my love of tacos, but I got the impression that wasn't what my little sister meant.

Was somebody going to ruin my love for tacos by associating it with a bad memory?

No. No. No. I'd had about enough. You can slug me in the face, try and blow me up, but take my tacos?

Not today, Satan.

Not today.

Hal pressed me for an answer. "Do tacos and the letters WIF mean anything to you?"

"Well, how do you mean, do tacos mean anything to me? They're part of my life force. That and Twinkies and Pop-Tarts and grape soda. I eat them a lot." I gave Win a guilty look. "Probably more than I should. What do you mean, do they mean anything to me?"

She swallowed hard and licked her dry lips. "Tacos. There was a man holding a tray of tacos. He was crying. Tino…Theo, maybe?"

"Tito?" I asked incredulously.

"Yes!" she said, her eyes blazing. "He was there. Dark hair, round face, Hispanic? Clear as day, and I got the impression he wanted to give you tacos."

My heart clenched in my chest. "That sure sounds like Tito. Tito owned a food truck. Tacos, enchiladas, nachos. Fabulous Mexican food. When I first moved back here to Eb Falls, he had good deals on tacos. Because they were so cheap, they were what kept me and Bel alive while I tried to figure out what to do with my life."

Gosh, I'll never forget Tito and how kind he was to me. That is, until he thought I'd murdered someone. But we'd made up and it was awesome...until he was killed.

She grabbed my hand with urgent pressure. "Is he alive? I can never remember the outcome of all your investigations."

I cocked my head, unsure where she was going. "No. He died. It was awful. His family was a mess, but they're doing well now. In fact, every Tuesday, as often as I can, I have their tacos for lunch. His sons took over the food truck."

"He was in this vision. He had a plate of tacos the size of my face. I got the impression he was bringing them to you."

"And?" I coaxed.

"And same thing as the bit with the Endicott guy, who you said was in jail. He was standing over your husk of a body, crying."

Was Tito somehow reaching out from the afterlife? "I don't get it, Hal. This vision makes zero sense. It could be past, but I wasn't dead in the past while Tito was alive. Can't be present because I'm not dead now, soul's still intact, and if it's future, you've got ghosts popping up in your visions."

"That's true. Usually the people in my visions are

already dead or might possibly die, but that's only if they're past or future visions. This has to be a future vision because in all of these, you're…"

"*Dead*," I said woodenly. I was wide awake now, my eyes still grainy but my pulse racing. "But wait, how does that explain Hank Endicott? He's alive and in prison. How is he standing over me in a hospital gown if he's alive and I'm dead? Tito, I sort of get. Maybe his ghost comes to see me *after* I die? He thought a good taco could make anything better. He always said that. So, I don't understand. Unless Endicott escapes prison the way Tammy did? But what are the chances of that happening with two of the cases I've been involved in, and if he escaped, why did he escape in a hospital gown?"

Hal scrunched her eyes shut. "I don't have any answers. I'm sorry, Stevie. It doesn't make any sense to me either.

"What did you mean by the letters WIF, Hal?" Win asked.

She tucked her hair behind her ears, her words filled with intensity. "On the ground next to Stevie's body, in the snow. Tito was crying tears and as the drops hit the freshly fallen snow, they formed the letters WIF."

WIF.

What in the Flying Wallendas was going on?

This got hinkier by the minute. "I have no idea what the letters mean. I don't think any investigation of a crime I've ever been involved with has been with someone with a name that starts with the letter WIF. First or last, but I'd have to go back over them to see. There've been a lot."

"Maybe it is anagram?" Arkady suggested.

"But no matter how you rearrange the letters, it doesn't spell anything.

"Listen, I got the impression Tito was desperately trying to warn you about something or wished he'd warned you sooner about something and it had to do with the letters WIF."

Somehow, Tito had pushed through the veil, just like Sophie, to warm me. I looked up at the ceiling then, my heart full. "Hey, Arkady, if you ever see Tito, tell him I said thank you."

"Dah, my sweet magnolia. I will, but I have not seen him. I have not seen anyone you scuffle with either. They wouldn't be on this plane. This place is full of only peace and serenity. The bad guys and criminals go somewhere else."

Exhaustion took over again. I was so tired from trying to figure out what was happening that every bone in my body felt like butter.

I let my head rest on the wood of the table and sighed. "I don't know what any of this means."

"And you won't tonight, poppet," Atti said, his deep voice, so funny to hear coming from such a tiny creature, soft and warm in my ear. "Say good night to your fiancé, it's bedtime for you."

"But—" I began to protest.

"No buts, dear child. Say you're good nights and off you shall go. I'll send Hal with you to stand guard."

I looked at Win. "You okay after tonight?"

He gave me a quick kiss and nuzzled my cheek. "I'm fine, Dove. Off with you now. My mate here is right. It's bedtime for all beautiful mediums."

I giggled as he pulled me upward and into his arms. "Do you know a lot of those?"

"Only the one who counts. Good night, my sweet Dove. Sleep the sleep of the angels," he whispered before Atti waved his wing and I was upstairs, in my pajamas and in my bed, feeling safer than I had all day.

Hal sat at the edge of my bed and smiled. "So this is the bed Win had built for you. It's like an enormous nook in the wall with a window facing the ocean. Really beautiful work, Stevie. You got yourself a good one, big sister."

I pulled the covers up under my chin and snuggled in, letting the sound of the waves crashing and the rain pelting the window soothe me. My heart glowed thinking about Win and how mad I was about him.

"The best. He's the best."

She leaned forward and kissed my forehead with a smile. "Indeedy. Now sleep. I'll be right here if you need me."

With that, she ran her index fingers over my eyes and they closed, and the last thing I remember was Whiskey jumping up on the bed and snuggling next to me the way he always did before, I drifted off into a dreamless sleep.

I woke to the smell of coffee and bacon and the wonderful feeling of being nurtured.

"Up and at 'em, Stevie," Hal called from outside the door, her husky voice cheerful. "Breakfast is in fifteen and Atti will have my head if I don't get you up and showered."

I groaned as I slid past Whiskey, my feet touching the floor. "Fifteen minutes isn't long enough for me to even brush my hair, let alone be showered and ready to go, Hal."

She poked her gorgeous face into the bedroom, fresh as a daisy, wearing a cute red slouchy hat and jeans fashionably ripped at the knees. "Try your magic, Stevie," she said with a mischievous smile. "It's just a snap of your fingers away."

I waved her off with a wry smile. "Yeah, yeah. I thought we weren't supposed to use our magic for personal gain."

Hal wrinkled her cute nose. "You're not buying a Gucci bag, silly. You're taking a magical shower and putting on clothes you bought yourself so you won't be late for breakfast."

I bit the inside of my cheek, nervous. "But what if I can't do it."

"Just try," she encouraged. "And if you can't, I'll stall the old curmudgeon."

Laughing, I nodded. "Tell Atti I won't miss breakfast —even if I have to do it with morning breath."

Hal took her leave and I trudged to the bathroom with Whiskey behind me.

I took a good long look at myself in the mirror, my hair—now well past my shoulders—smushed to the side of my face, yesterday's mascara leaving me with racoon eyes.

My pajamas were wrinkled and my one eye still had quite a bruise. But my leg looked okay. The bullet Tammy had shot at me the other day hadn't left much of a mark.

How many people get up in the morning and say something like that as though it were normal?

Hey, how was your day, yesterday?

Eh, yesterday wasn't too bad. I was only shot. Just a small scratch, no big deal.

Sighing, I couldn't really remember if there was a spell for hygiene, but I closed my eyes, gripped the edge of my bright white sink and thought about what I had to wear in my closet.

The day was typically gloomy for February in Washington, and from the looks of it, windy. That meant a dress was out, but a turtleneck and some jeans would do.

I decided against heels for some cute work boots instead, in case I had to run for my life, which didn't feel like an impossibility after the last couple days or so.

I closed my eyes, saw my outfit and what I'd like to look like in my mind's eye, and snapped my fingers. When I opened them, I grinned.

I'd done it!

My hair was brushed and curled in soft waves, sweeping across my forehead, a miracle all unto itself. My makeup was in place, hiding my bruise as best it could, and when I ran my tongue over my teeth, they felt clean as a whistle. I even had a pair of my hoop earrings on and my favorite perfume.

Hah!

"Well, would you look at you," Bel crooned as he swooped into the room. "I smell it. You used your magic to shower and dress, didn't you, Boss?"

I couldn't stop smiling. "I did! And best of all, it worked! No weird, half-baked results. Just exactly what I pictured in my mind."

Bel buzzed to my shoulder and looked at my reflection. "And ya look pretty as a picture. Now get your gears grinding. Atticus made a quiche and brioche French toast and all sorts of things. I get the feeling he doesn't like to be kept waiting."

He pecked my cheek and called to Whiskey for breakfast while I took one last look at myself before I headed downstairs, too, feeling hopeful.

So hopeful.

I skipped down the steps, my heart glowing in my chest, only to be greeted by some serious sourpusses around the kitchen table. As I walked into the kitchen and saw the beautiful spread Atti had prepared, the vibe I got was dreary at best.

I approached, knowing my happy bubble was about to break. "Guys, what's up?"

Win held his hand out to me and I walked toward him, grabbing it. He pulled me close, his arm around my waist. "It's Hank Endicott."

I swallowed. "What about him?" I asked, my voice shaky.

Hal looked at me, her face filled with sympathy. "He died yesterday morning, Stevie. In the prison infirmary. Of a heart attack."

CHAPTER 14

I sat down in a chair, my legs trembling, all my happiness about my magical accomplishment evaporating into the air.

When I was finally able to speak, I took a deep breath. "So when you had the vision, Endicott was already dead. Which could mean you're seeing a future vision. One where I'm dead and my soul is gone."

But Hal shook her head with determination. "Not necessarily. I've stopped a person or two from hurting themselves when I knew the vision I had might bring them harm."

"But they weren't already dead. You prevented them from harming themselves. There's a difference. Endicott is *dead*."

Hal slapped her hand on the table, making us all jump. "There is no difference, Stevie Cartwright! I've prevented deaths, and if I have to, I'll prevent yours. Do you hear me? I won't let anyone hurt you!"

I let out a shaky breath, my appetite all but gone. "I know you'd never let anyone hurt me, Hal. But you could get hurt here, too. I mean, you're only one witch up against…what? We don't know. We don't know how strong Sal is, we don't know what else he's capable of. We don't know who else or how many people he's convinced to help him. It's been like an all-star game of People Stevie Put In Jail Fight Back these last couple of days. He's proving to be a force to be reckoned with. I won't let you end up hurt because of my beef with a dead guy that you had nothing to do with. You have to go home."

I said it and I meant it. If something happened to my sister because she was involved with me, I'd die.

Hal's eyes narrowed and her glossed lips thinned. "First, that's not going to happen. So don't even speak the words again or I'll sew your mouth shut with my magic needle until this is over. Got that? Second, yes. I'm only one lowly witch with sometimes wonky powers, but I've gotten myself and others out of some pretty serious jams all on my own. So forget me going anywhere. Now quiet your face and have some French toast."

She grabbed the serving handle from one of our white CorningWare dishes and plopped some on the plate in front of me, shoving the fresh maple syrup toward me.

When I didn't move, she glared. "Eat. You'll need energy if we're going to figure out how to stop this Sal Finch from taking you out."

Atti flew to the spot on the table next to Hal's plate. "Now, poppet, mind your temper, please. Your sister's only thinking of you. What kind of sister would she be if she didn't put you before here in an instance like this?"

Shoving some scrambled eggs into her mouth, Hal shook her head. "Don't you tell me to mind anything. We're sisters. If Mom and Nana Karen taught me anything, it's that you don't ever leave family behind. You're there for each other no matter what. Now no more talk about leaving. No one's going anywhere."

I reached across the table and grabbed her hand. "Hal. I'm sorry. I didn't mean to insult you. We're not talking everyday criminals. We're talking ghostly criminals. I love you. I would never want to hurt your feelings…but this is dangerous."

She took a sip of orange juice and eyed me over the rim of her glass. "And so is walking across the street. Look, Stevie, I know you're worried we'll get hurt, but not half as worried as I am that you'll die. Do you *want* to die? I'm sorry I lost my temper, but there's no way I'm leaving. Oh, and I can't find this Winnie anywhere. I popped into Paris early this morning and no one was home. So let's scratch her off our list for the moment."

I hadn't been able to get in touch with Winnie either. I didn't understand it. "I can't find her either."

Hal bobbed her head. "Okay then, what's our next plan of action until we hear from either Dad or Atti's friend with a better spell to force this guy out into the open?"

I can't tell you how afraid I was for both Hal and Atti, but I'd do the same, even without any powers. I'd stay and fight it out with her—beside her. It made me wish I'd known her mother Keeva. She'd instilled a sense of family in Hal I wasn't accustomed to.

Growing up, it was just me and Dita, and though now she was a pretty good mother, back then, she'd been the worst. It had always been mostly me and Bel. He was my babysitter, my cinnamon toast maker, my confidant, my guide.

He was the only support I'd had.

"I think we need to talk to Edmund, don't you, Dove? Maybe he'll remember something the others haven't," Win suggested, smoothing over the rough edges of our argument with his dulcet tones.

I put some French toast in my mouth and nodded.

It was really all we had in the way of a lead to try and save my soul.

I wasn't sure how we'd be greeted at Adele's flower shop today. Yesterday, she'd looked at me as though I was the devil himself. Hal said it was some kind of spell. I could only pray it had worn off and we'd go back to being friendly acquaintances again.

I waved to her as I pushed open the glass door at Flower Power, and thankfully she waved back, with enthusiasm, no less. Surrounded by her refrigerated cases of colorful flowers and various knickknacks and vases, she was her usual happy, grinning self again.

She glided across the floor and reached out to give me a warm hug. "Stevie, how are you?"

I think all three of us were taken aback, but Hal mouthed from behind me, "Told you it was a spell."

I hugged her back, relishing the scent of roses in her hair. "I'm good, Adele. Do you mind if I talk to Edmund?"

She flapped her hands at me and looked astonished. "Of course not, sugarbuns. Why would I?"

Okay, yeah. This was nuttypants. "I just want to ask him about the flowers he delivered to me yesterday."

She cocked her head at me much like she had the day before, only today, she didn't appear to be afraid. "Edmund wasn't even in yesterday, Stevie. How could he have delivered flowers to you?"

Now we were all in a state of shock, but I had to pat us on the back for hiding it as well as we did. "But he did. Ask Brenda," I said, pointing to the tall girl at one of the workstations making an amazing arrangement of roses.

She wiped her hands on her apron and strode over, giving us a half smile of curiosity. "Ask me what?"

"The arrangement of flowers you made for me yesterday. Don't you remember talking to me about them?"

Brenda shook her head. "I don't…

I was hearing her correctly, right? She was telling us she didn't make me an arrangement of flowers.

"Are you sure?" I asked, trying to hide my disbelief.

Brenda drove her hands into the pockets of her apron. "I swear didn't make an arrangement for you, Miss Cartwright. Maybe it was Leah?"

Leah was Adele's other employee. She was at a table near Brenda's and she shook her sandy-blonde head. "It wasn't me."

"Let me check my orders from yesterday," Adele offered. "Wait right there, gorgeous." She went to the long glass case that held her cash register and iPad and began flipping through the screen.

"This is crazy. Did we fall into another dimension?" I whispered to Hal and Win.

But Hal shook her head. "No. Someone put a spell on them and they don't remember anything. I knew it. You'll see. Adele will tell you there was no order sent to you yesterday in three, two—"

"Nothing here, Stevie. Maybe it came from another shop in the town over?" Adele suggested with a frown. But then she smiled. "Neither here nor there. A pretty girl should always have flowers, no matter where they come from."

I didn't know what to say, I was so astonished. It was as though yesterday never happened.

Win stepped in. "You're absolutely right. A pretty girl should always have flowers, that's why I always order them from you, Adele. Because I know you'll send nothing but the absolute best."

Adele giggled and swatted Win's arm with a flirty

wink. "Oh, you." Then she shrugged in sympathy. "Sorry I couldn't help you, honey."

"No worries. Any ideas about where to find Edmund? Is he on a delivery?"

"Today's his other day off, but lemme think. Hmmm," she said, tapping her chin with a pink-tipped nail. "If I know that boy, he's over at that new gym doing reps or some such exercise. Seems he spends all his time there these days, bulking up."

I gripped her arm in a warm embrace. "Thanks again, Adele. Good to see you."

"You, too, honey. Bye now."

As we walked back outside into the gloom of the day, I almost couldn't speak. I stood dumbfounded on the sidewalk. This was some powerful spell for a guy who could barely pull it together enough to kill me the right way.

What had Sal Finch been doing up in the afterlife for all this time? Studying possession and witchcraft?

Hal took my freezing-cold hand in her warmer one. "Don't fret."

"How can I help *but* fret, Hal? I feel like I'm in the twilight zone."

"That's because you're not used to the ways of the witch anymore. My life is like this all the time. Now that your powers are coming back, you'd better start adjusting."

Win put his arm at my elbow as fat, fluffy snowflakes started to fall. "Come, Dove. Let's head over to Cardio Cave and fish about for Edmund, yes?"

I nodded silently and began to follow them down the block and to the left. Cardio Cave's was new, and had become a real hangout for the local kids on the football team. It had all the latest equipment and classes—they even had goat yoga.

As we walked and the snowflakes fell, I almost smiled. I loved the snow. If it weren't for my life here, I'd move to Maine to be closer to my sister and even *more* snow.

As though she'd read my mind, Hal smiled. "It's beautiful, isn't it?"

I sighed. "I love the snow. We've had more than the norm this year. Most people hate it because they don't want to drive in it, but not me. It makes me happy."

"Me, too. I can't imagine living where there's no snow or the leaves don't change. I love visiting tropical places, but Maine will always have my heart."

It made me sad we'd likely never be neighbors. She had a business in Maine and employees who counted on her, and I had Madam Z's.

Tucking her close, I squeezed her to my side. "I know. That's why I'm glad we have Zoom."

She chuckled as we reached the door to Cardio Cave and Win pulled it open. "If you get your magic back, you can pop in anytime."

If...

The scent of deodorant, sweat and heavy-duty sanitizer hit me in the face with a hearty slap. The music was loud and abrasive and meant to inspire, I suppose, but it was an easy tell I was getting older because it hurt my ears.

Win frowned. "I can't hear myself think in here. Does no one consider Mozart a worthy workout playlist?"

I laughed as we strolled toward a bank of ellipticals and treadmills, filled with those dedicated to exercising.

The weight machines were in the back, clanking and pounding as grunts filled the air. Win spotted Edmund, working his arms on some contraption with pulleys.

"There he is. After you, ladies," he said, sweeping his arm.

We made our way over to Edmund, wearing shorts and a sweaty gray T-shirt bearing his high school logo. We passed two of the Bustamante brothers on our way. Mateo and Juan Filipe, each on a treadmill, laughing and talking. I gave them a quick wave and a smile, remembering what Hal had said about their stepfather, Tito, my heart clenching.

As we approached Edmund, perspiration dotted his brow and his face was red from tugging the pulleys.

When he saw us, much like everyone else today, he let the pulleys go and smiled. "Hey, Miss Cartwright, Mr. Winningham. How are you guys?" He gave Halliday a curious look, but being the polite boy he was, just said, "I'd offer to shake your hand, but I'm kinda sweaty. I'm Edmund. Nice to meet you."

"Halliday Valentine. Stevie's sister."

He nodded, planting his hands on his hips. "Aw, yeah. I just remembered she said she had a sister she'd found recently. That's really nice."

"Hey, Edmund, we won't take up much of your time, but may I ask you a question?"

He grinned his boyish grin, wiping his forehead with the towel around his neck. "'Course you can, Miss Cartwright. No trouble at all."

Yesterday he'd been running down my porch steps to get away from me as though the hounds of Hell were at nipping at his heels, and today he was treating me like an old friend.

Though, this poor boy had now been used by more than one spirit. When all was said and done, I'd have to ask Hal to put some kind of protection spell on him. He was too kind, too open to keep an evil spirit at bay.

I looked around at all the mirrors and the people working out and kept my voice low—or as low as I could with the music blasting. "First, just call me Stevie, please. Second, do you recall delivering flowers to me yesterday?"

He, like everyone else, gave me a confused look. "No. It wasn't me; I didn't even work yesterday."

Hal took a deep whiff next to him—brave if you ask me, considering the stench of sweat—and nodded behind his back. *Spell,* she mouthed.

I guess I hadn't expected much, but I'd hoped. Turned out, that hope was futile. "You don't remember seeing me at all yesterday? Coming to the house?"

He frowned and shook his head. "No, ma'am. Did

someone deliver flowers to you and you thought I'd delivered them?"

I stared at him for a minute, not meaning to, lost in thought, and he squirmed.

"Miss Cartwright…er, Stevie?"

I pulled my crossbody purse over in front of my belly as though I needed to protect myself from something. What else was there to ask, really? He wouldn't remember anything anyway.

"Sorry, Edmund. Yes. Someone did deliver flowers to me. Must have been a mix-up. Either way, thanks for your time."

"You bet." He hitched his thumb over his shoulder at the rowing machine. "I gotta get back to it before I lose my steam. Do you mind?"

"Not at all," Win said, giving him a slap on the back. "Enjoy your workout. Come, Dove. Let's go, shall we?"

I nodded. "You guys start and I'll catch up. I have to use the ladies' room."

"Um, no. We'll wait right here," Hal said firmly. "In fact, I'll come with. Win, you wait here for us."

I rolled my eyes, but my bladder was full from the gallon of coffee I drank before leaving the house in the hopes of settling my nerves. "Fine, c'mon."

We wove our way through the various workout machines and past a shelf of yoga balls, toward a long hall where the ladies' room was located.

As we pushed the doors open, I headed for a stall, and so did Hal. It didn't appear as though anyone else was about, so I said from my stall, "You know what I was wondering, Hal?"

"What?"

I looked at the door of the stall thoughtfully. "However the flowers got to me is inconsequential at this point. What I want to know is, how did Sal know what my favorite flowers are to begin with? It's super personal."

"Maybe he asked around upstairs? Those you-know-whatsits that showed up last night sure seemed to scurry like ants doused with water when Sal's name was mentioned. Maybe he talked to them?"

They sure had. "I don't get that, either. Has he suddenly become king of the afterlife or something? Why is everyone so afraid of him?"

I heard the toilet flush and then the water in the sink run just as I was buttoning my jeans. "Beats me," Hal responded. "But they sure did—hey! Who do you think you are? This is the ladies' room. Get out!"

And then there was a thud, and I saw Hal's legs, sprawled out on the floor from under the stall, her red snow boots visible seconds before someone bashed in my door, scooped me up by the front of my jacket and yanked me out to press me against the outside of the stall.

My mouth fell open as I hung there, my feet dangling freely, while Juan Felipe Bustamante held me by my neck with his enormous hands, against the wall and squeezed.

CHAPTER 15

His beautifully boned face, hard and chiseled, his coal-black eyes vacant, Juan Felipe said in a dead voice, *"He's coming, Stevie. Sal said he's coming because he owes you one!"*

I thought my eyeballs might pop right out of my head, he squeezed so hard, and truthfully, it had been a while since I'd had a go 'round with a bad guy. Meaning, all of my Mini-Spy moves took the exit-stage-left door...but only for a moment before I became really angry.

I'd been cracked in the face, almost blown up, and now someone was trying to strangle me to death, all because Sal had grown a set bigger than all of the afterlife.

I knew Juan Felipe was under some kind of spell, and this wasn't something he'd ever do under normal circumstances, but by golly, a girl only had so much she could take before she cracked.

And I cracked like the shell of an egg dropped on the floor.

As I struggled against him, my eyes almost rolling to the back of my head, I began to taunt my nemesis. "Is that you in there, Sal? Can't find a host body? Too weak?" I squeaked, which only made him squeeze harder.

Wrapping my hands around his wrists, I swung my knee and rammed it upward between his thighs, making him yelp, his perfect face scrunching in pain.

While he curled inward, loosening his grip just a little, I hated to do it—but I grabbed either side of his head and drove my thumbs into his eyes, all the while taunting him as best I could with his strong hands still around my neck. I didn't want to gouge his eyes out, just make him ease up, but if I had to, I would.

He howled his displeasure, loosening his grip just a little more.

"C'mon, Sal! Come and get me, you sore loser! You big scaredy cat!" I huffed out, my voice scratchy and strained.

He became angrier then, moving his hands up my neck until they were right under my chin, and then he began banging the back of my head against the wall.

"You did this!" he bellowed in my face. "You did this to me! You must pay! I want you dead—broken and battered and dead, dead, *dead*! Soulless for eternity!"

Vaguely, those words sounded familiar, but trust and believe, this wouldn't be the first time someone had said they wanted me dead.

The words didn't matter. The fact that I was going to have a crushed pharynx—that could be a problem.

Yet, his words didn't just sound familiar, they left me irate. So angry, so filled with rage, I screamed back as I tore at Juan Felipe's hair, "You wanna play? Then let's do this!"

Big words for someone who had little resources, but listen, I really believe you have to walk into a room like you own the joint and show no fear.

The very second I said those words was the very second everything around us exploded.

The doors of the stalls blew open, the long mirror above the sinks shattered and crashed all around us. The hand dryer flew from the wall and toilet paper ripped from the silver boxes that held the rolls, clanging to the ground.

I took that as an opportunity to use to my advantage.

With every last ounce of strength I had, I bashed my forehead against Juan Felipe's, head butting him with all my might.

He stumbled backward, just enough for me to drop to the tile floor before I heard, "Evil be gone from this place! Evil no longer show your face!"

Hal!

With a snap of her fingers, everything stopped. Toilet paper floated to the ground, peeled paint rolled off the stalls in sheets.

I scrambled up and ran to the other end of the bathroom, my feet crunching over shattered glass, I grabbed her by the shoulders then ran my hands over her face, already bruised and swollen. "Hal, are you all right?"

She pulled me into a tight hug before setting me from her, her hands gripping my forearms. "I'm fine. Are *you* okay? Who's he?" she asked, pointing to Juan Felipe, crumbled on the floor.

I disengaged from her hug and knelt beside Juan. "Oh, cheese and rice! He's Tito's son. But wait—before you blow him out of the water with one of your spells for choking me, the same thing happened with him that happened with everyone else. I don't think he knew what he was doing because Sal was possessing him."

Her beautiful blue eyes flew open wide. "Sweet pizza rolls," she mumbled.

As we stood there, and the loud music blared—music, I suppose, we should be thankful for, now that I'd blown up the ladies' room—I looked all around the space, then at Hal.

And my sister knew exactly what I wanted. "I'll fix this. Don't worry. It'll be like it never happened." Closing her eyes and snapping her fingers, she muttered something in Latin, and in seconds, the room was back in order.

Going back to Juan Felipe, I knelt again and brushed his ebony-black hair from his slack face. His eyes were red somethin' awful, and blood dripped from the corner of one.

"And Juan Felipe?"

"I can fix that, too, also like it never happened." Good to her promise, she snapped her fingers again—and all of a sudden, he sat bolt upright. But he didn't look at either of us.

Instead, he rose and looked toward the door, before he cracked his knuckles and pushed his way out.

"Will he remember?" I asked, my voice scratchy and husky from my throat being squeezed.

She shook her head, bending to grab her hat. "Nope, and I can tell you why."

"Why?" I asked, feeling tremendous guilt about her face.

Her face took on a look of hesitant worry. "Because the magic used to turn him into a vessel? It's some of the worst kind of magic that's ever existed, Stevie. It's insidious. He smelled so bad, I could have choked on the stench. I won't lie. We have real trouble here."

Oh.

Good to know.

We were right back where we started from, sitting at the kitchen table after spending an entire day coming up with absolutely nothing while we waited for Atti's connection to get back to us.

Hal scrolled her phone as I sat by the windows and watched the day wane and descend into the early fog of evening.

Atti was busy tending to a beef stew he'd had simmering all day while Belfry and Whiskey napped.

Strike had finally decided I wasn't so bad after all and sat on my lap, even though I'd cremated a gym bathroom and almost took out someone I like very much.

Hal had used her magic to clean up the mess I'd made in the bathroom and of poor Juan Felipe. As we left the gym, my jacket closed around my neck to hide the bruising and Hal with her head down, Juan and Mateo had waved at us and smiled as if the former had never tried to choke me to death.

All I kept thinking about was the words Juan Felipe had said. Sal wanted me dead, broken, battered, and soulless. No one else had said that, but it didn't add up to much if you looked at the bigger picture. He'd made all sorts of threats. The threats *did* add up to something. Me dead.

I tried to focus on any one clue, but nothing was sticking. I was waffling something fierce.

Suddenly, Hal sat up straight, putting her phone down on the kitchen table. "Hallie-Oop," she muttered.

"Pardon?" Win said, lifting his eyes from the laptop screen where he scrolled aimlessly.

She jumped up and began to pace, her booted feet clomping across the hardwood. "Hallie-Oop! Egan Joseph, when he was possessed by that fruit salad, he called me Hallie-Oop. No one calls me that but very few people, and they're all in Maine. How would Sal know my nickname?"

Now I sat up, too, straightening in my chair and setting Strike on the floor. "But what does that mean to us?"

"What it means is, how does Sal know what people call me? Do we have a mutual ghostly friend who told him? You've never called me that in person or even in a Zoom call, Stevie. So how did Sal know about it?"

Atti flew to the table, waving his wing to make three place settings appear. "I hate to tell you this, pet, but that feels like an awfully weak clue."

She sat back down and sighed. "I don't mean it's a clue so much as I mean, maybe it's a connection? Maybe someone I know has been yakking it up with good ol' Sal and they can give us some kind of information that we haven't been able to get our hands on, since no one remembers Sal's existence once he's wreaked his havoc."

"So do you know anyone who's died who called you that?" I wondered out loud.

She pinched her temples and scrunched her eyes tight before opening them and looking at me with a pained expression. "My mother. She called me that all the time."

Oh, sweet mother of pearl. If Hal's mother Keeva's spirit was mixed up in this, I'd simply die. I licked my dry lips nervously. "Oh, Hal…"

My stomach was in turmoil, my head felt like it might explode. I didn't know what to say.

"No, no," she said, shaking her head. "Don't do that, Stevie. My mother was one of the toughest witches I've ever known. Don't think for a second she couldn't handle Sal. If he somehow got that information from her, it wasn't without a helluva fight. Aside from that, I can still feel her with me. Her soul's intact."

Relief washed over me in waves, my panic subsiding a little. I sent a mental thank you to the universe.

"Of course it is, Poppet," Atti soothed in deep tones. "My Keeva was a superior witch. She'd never let her soul be stolen by some hooligan like Sal Finch!"

I toyed with the cloth napkin, putting it in my lap as Atti served us each a steaming bowl of stew filled with bright orange carrots, creamy white potatoes and tender chunks of meat. "Is there anyone else you can think of?"

She closed her eyes and let her head tip backward on her shoulders. "Nope. Everyone else is still alive. So if he got that information from them, he did it the way he did with the others and they won't remember anyway."

Win ran a hand through his thick dark hair while he let his stew cool. "You know what I'm still curious about, Stephania? How, in all the world, has Sal gained so much afterlife traction? Has it changed that much since I left? I realize it's possible he was willing to do plenty of things I wouldn't in order to get back here, but the traction he's gained is incredible."

Shrugging, I rubbed my sore neck. "I was wondering the same thing. What were some of the things the spirits wanted you to do? Is it like the afterlife mob?"

Arkady's laugh was deep and hearty. "It can be very much like Russian mob. Many bad spirits offer many schemes and enticements to get back to your plane, but it is all scam."

Win swirled his glass of wine, the burgundy liquid sloshing against th sides. "What Arkady said. There are as many untrustworthy spirits upstairs as there are here on this plane, Dove."

"Good to know. So moving along, what do the letters WIF mean, and why am I suddenly seeing and hearing ghosts? Everything is topsy-turvy all over. I feel like my whole world has tipped upside down."

"Eat, Poppet," Atti ordered. "You must be strong while we explore everything. That's how you do it, isn't it?"

I took a spoonful of his heavenly stew and nodded. "That's how we usually do it, but I'm not typically the person someone's after."

"Not true, strawberry shortcake," Arkady reminded me. "You have been chased almost more than most spies Arkady Bagrov knows."

I laughed, making my throat sting and my head hurt. "I meant I'm not usually the star of the investigation. This is too close and too personal and I'm having trouble getting perspective."

Win ran his hand gently over my bruised throat. "You should have let Hal heal that for you."

I shook my head. "Nope. I want to remember what's happening to me and this is a perfect reminder. Plus, I want to be able to do it myself."

"Atta girl," Atti cheered. "Now eat and nourish yourself. You look like a wet noodle that's been pulled through a keyhole. Also, I cooked all day. I *and* my cuisine need appreciation."

Hal laughed and shook her napkin at him. "You did not, Atticus Finch. You used your magic to make it smell like you slaved over a hot stove, but what you really did is waved your wings and boom—delicious stew to rival the Barefoot Contessa's."

He swatted playfully at her. "You hush, fresh one. There are no tears of virgin geese in it or homemade mayonnaise."

"Do virgin geese truly exist, mate?" Win asked him with a hearty chuckle.

We all started to laugh. I guess the long day and all of the fear and worry had begun to get to us and we needed a release.

Tears fell down my cheeks at the thought of virgin geese as I snorted and snuffed until Atti suddenly cleared his throat, grabbing our attention.

"Children! I've just received two text messages, one from my dear friend, and one from home. Two things. First, we have a spell to draw out this ghastly Sal, and something to contain him in—forever. Almost like a Pandora's box that must never be opened. But this isn't an easy spell, and it must be done at a precise time of day and in a precise location."

I'd roll my eyes, but one still hurt. Typical witchery at its finest. There was always a string attached. "So we have to stand on our heads during a three-quarter moon in a valley of wildflowers and spit nickels out of our noses in order to catch the jerk, right?"

Hal snickered.

But Atti didn't. "No nickels. I believe it's quarters."

Hal laughed out loud, as did Win, covering their mouths with their napkins.

"It's nothing like that, pet, but you do know what witchcraft is like. It has its quirks," Atti reminded me.

That it did. I set my spoon down and looked at his tiny green and red body, standing in the middle of my table as though he were ten feet tall, and agreed. "Okay, fine. I'll get my bongo drums and braid my hair. I'll do whatever it takes to get rid of Sal. Now, what's number two?"

He held up his wing and read the rest of the message from Hal's phone. "It's Karen, Halliday."

And I didn't like how he said it. He sounded morose and hesitant.

Hal jumped up as though she was too afraid to look at her phone. "Nana? What's wrong? Did she eat too many candy canes again? I swear, she's forever trying to talk Hobbs into giving her candy canes. I know he wouldn't because he knows she has to watch her sugar. So she's sneaking them from somewhere. That woman is going to be the death of me—"

"Halliday!" Atticus called out, rising to meet her eyes. "Listen carefully to me. Karen is missing."

My heart thudded against my ribs as I rose, too, griping Hal's shoulder.

"Hobbs said there's a message in the barn, scratched out on her stall."

No, no, no, no, no! I silently shouted out to the universe.

"What does it say, Atti?" I asked, my throat tight and sorer than ever.

There was a moment of silence while Atti inhaled. I heard the sharp wheeze of it as we all held our breath.

Then he said, "It says, 'tell Hallie-Oop I send my regards.'"

CHAPTER 16

My knees nearly buckled and Win made a grab for me to keep me from falling to the ground. I held onto Hal, who also lost her footing, gripping the back of the kitchen table chair.

She leaned against me before taking a long, deep breath, and then she turned around, her face red, her eyes glittering. "I'll kill whoever took her. I'll send them so deep into the universe, they'll never, ever find their way back to a plane—to *any* plane ever again! And I'll make it hurt. I'll peel their skin off, layer by layer until they beg for mercy, and then I'll peel another layer off—"

"Hal!" Win called out, letting me go in favor of gripping her shoulders and giving her a light shake. "Stop. Listen to me. You must not allow your emotions to get the better of you here. We need the whole picture and the whole picture requires you to listen, stay on your toes, and make a plan."

Her chest heaved, rising and falling in anger, but she appeared to be able to focus on Win and listen.

"Better?" he asked, letting her go.

Hal licked her lips and sucked in her cheeks. "If better means ready to calmly kill someone, then I'm better."

Atticus clucked his tongue. "Halliday, Winterbottom is correct. You must have your wits about you and keep focus. It's the first rule of witchcraft. Do not give in to your emotions. I beg of you."

She took more deep breaths, her cheeks puffing in and out. "I'm sorry. You're right, Atti, and I have a plan. Maybe she's just missing and it has nothing to do with magic at all? You know how she's always disappearing," she said, and the hope in her voice heart tore at mine.

"But the message scratched into her stall said, 'Tell Hallie-Oop I send my regards,'" Win reminded her. "I don't wish to be the bearer of bad news, but we must assess the evidence, not what we wish to be so."

Win was in spy mode now and Arkady followed right behind him. "Dah, pretty lady. Facts are important. Do not allow your emotions to get better of you. Keep head on straight."

She pointed upward, and I saw she was fighting tears. "You're right, Arkady. So here's what I'm going to do. I'm going to zip myself to the barn and sniff around. See if it was the same magic I smelled in the bathroom at that smelly gym."

I began to say, "Hal let me go with—"

But she was gone in the blink of any eye.

"He has Karen. That's how he found out what Hal's nickname is. He took Karen," I said, my voice shaking with rage. "*Sal took Karen.*"

Win wrapped his arm around my waist. "Likely, that's the case, but we don't know that for sure and there's hope, Dove. Let's look at what we do know. Atticus's connection offered us a spell. We'll use it and we'll find Nana Karen."

My stomach sloshed and wobbled, the acidic feel of burning doom in its pit. I gripped Win's hand as the magnitude of it all set it. "I did this. This is because of me, and I won't be able to stand it if Karen is hurt because of me, Win!"

"Boss! Breathe," Bel said in my ear as he landed on my shoulder. "This isn't your fault. This is that cuckoocake's fault. Now *stop*. Get a grip, and be ready to help your sister make a plan. We need a plan to lure this zippety-do-dah out and get rid of him—for good."

"Belfry's right, Dove. Let's start thinking rationally and make a plan. Please. You must get hold of yourself."

Atti flew into my line of sight, his tiny wings flapping madly. "I know you're terrified for your sister, but if this Sal truly does have Karen? He'll send her back. Anyone with only half a brain would send her back. Her mouth alone is enough to drive a man insane."

In the middle of all this turmoil, I couldn't help but laugh at his words. "That's so mean, Atti. She's so sweet."

"Hah! There isn't a sweet bone in that woman's body, and while I adore her, something she must never know or she'll have the upper hand, she's as sweet as vinegar."

Then reality set back in and I swallowed hard, my throat raspy and dry. Taking a swig of the bottle of wine, I looked to Atti. "Okay, big girl knickers on. Tell me what we have to do in order to draw this jerkface out and send him to the outer stratospheres of Mars."

"It won't be easy, Stephania. It's an advanced spell. Far more advanced than either Halliday or myself have been privy to. It's one that cannot be dithered about. It must be swift and clean. Bah! I truly wish I could locate Baba Yaga, it would make everything so much—"

"Wait." I held up a hand. "You tried to contact Baba? You know how she feels about me, Atti. You know what she did to me. How could you ask her to help me?"

He lifted his tiny beak with clear indignance. "I did, and I won't apologize. She's the strongest witch I know and has the ability to put a stop to this nonsense. Surely your pride isn't bigger than saving yourself and the people around you, is it?"

I let my head hang low, feeling guilty for putting my pride first. "I'm sorry. That was selfish of me. Of course not. But I bet you got a big fat nothing but a wall of silence, didn't you?"

"'Tis true. I've heard nothing from her and there isn't another witch I can think of who'd be willing to go up against whatever we appear to be faced with."

His stark honesty struck a chord in me, making it harder for me to keep my tears in check. People were getting hurt. People I loved, and still, no one would help.

I swallowed back my tears, fighting off my feelings of betrayal that simply wouldn't go away. "Because it's me, right? Because it's bad Stevie Cartwright who broke the rules and everyone's afraid they'll be punished because I've been shunned—even people who aren't in my coven. Am I wrong?"

Atti sighed. "You're not wrong, pet. But I'm willing, and so is Halliday. You have us. You'll *always* have us."

Boy, this was some mess, but I would not allow this sick entity to hurt the people I love. "So tell me what we have to do. I'll do whatever it takes to get Karen back and get rid of Sal."

Hal magically reappeared in a thin mist of pink, her face wracked in anguish. "It was definitely the same magic, so I'm going to assume it's the same perp. I took a picture of what that scum wrote." She scrolled her phone and showed us.

I blanched, all the blood draining from my face. "So she's really gone?" I whispered.

Hal narrowed her eyes, but she lifted her chin with determination. "Yes. She's gone. Hobbs said he hasn't seen her since yesterday afternoon. He had a meeting in Bangor overnight, so he left his dog with a sitter. When he went to check on her this morning, she wasn't there. Despite the message, he looked all over Marshmallow Hollow for her before texting me." Hal pulled off her hat and ran a hand through her hair in frustration. "Dang it, I should have at least checked on her while I was here. It only takes a minute, for spit's sake. If only because she's always getting into something."

"Then we shall assume Sal has her in some capacity. But it can't be easy to hide a reindeer, Halliday," Win insisted, his jaw clenching, his tone no-nonsense. "First we need to find him and then we need to force him to tell us where Karen is."

Hal's nod was curt. "Right. So what's this spell and what do we have to do to get her back and get him away from Stevie?"

Atti waved us all to the table. "Sit. I shall make coffee and we'll discuss."

Hal crossed her arms over her chest. "Which means this isn't going to be pretty."

"It's the blimey mother of all containment spells, Halliday," Atti confirmed. "But first, we must lure him to us. We must entice his corporeal being away from the plane and through the veil. That will be the real trick."

"And we do that how?" I asked on a squeak.

Hal made a face. "And does it involve a cauldron and lots of bubbling liquid, because I'm sure you remember how that went when I was seven and I got hold of Mom's book of spells."

Atti barked a laugh. "I do. There was green goo everywhere. Alas, no cauldron, Halliday. Not this time. No, this time we're using an evocation spell, and it involves an intricate diagram drawn upon the ground by a particular deciduous tree facing due north when the moon is five minutes after at its highest point in the night sky. Then we'll need incense, your wand…oh, and a dagger, of course."

As I listened, I thought duh. Why would it be something simple like standing in front of Arby's drive-thru at noon and ordering a roast beef and cheddar sandwich while you sang the National Anthem.

I don't know why I said it, but it was the first thing that popped into my head. "Do you know how many deciduous trees are in Washington State? Let alone Eb Falls? How do we know we have the right one?"

Atticus waved his wing and said, "Fear not, dear child."

In the middle of the table, a shiny gold compass appeared, along with a hand-carved ivory box—the one I assumed was meant to capture evil Sal and keep him in it forever—and a piece of parchment paper.

My mouth was so dry, I took the bottle of wine from the table again and had another gulp. "And when do we do this? Tonight when the moon is at its highest point?"

Because I wanted to get this the heck over with so we could either go back to living our lives or ending mine.

"Yes, pet. Tonight when the moon is five minutes after its highest point, which as you know, is midnight, or twelve-o-five."

Inhaling, I took deep, cleansing breaths and squared my shoulders. No way was I going to live my life like this, and no way was I going to let a douchcanoe like

Sal make it as miserable as possible without fighting back.

No way.

Looking at the microwave clock, I saw it was already eight p.m. Who knew how far away this deciduous tree was? What if this deciduous tree was in Nova Scotia? Or Ireland? Or who knew where.

As though she read my mind, Hal said gently, "I'll get us there, Stevie. No matter where it is. But I'd bet a case of my favorite wine and my right finger it's somewhere around here. Don't ghosts have limited capacity to roam?"

I shook my head in confusion. "I have no idea anymore. I don't know what they have or what they don't have. So much has changed in the afterlife since I had my powers. When I had them, if you'd told me Karen could come back as a reindeer and Win could possess an actual body, I would have told you that you were bananapants. But now? I don't know anymore."

Hal tapped the table with her fingernail. "We still haven't figured out how Nana Karen came back in the body of a reindeer, but I don't question it. I'll take her any way I can get her. Which means we need to figure out this spell, make a plan, and make sure we have everything as foolproof as possible. We can't afford any mistakes or to miss our window of opportunity."

"This is a portal, isn't it, Atti?" Bel asked on a tiny shiver. "We're opening a portal to call him out?"

"Essentially, yes, and it's dangerous to say the least."

"Meaning?" I asked. "How dangerous is dangerous?

I mean there are levels of dangerous. Say, on a scale of one to ten."

Atti rasped a sigh. "Do you want the truth?"

"With a side of honesty," I replied, my chin lifting.

"If we don't get this done, and done properly, pet, we'll unleash goddess knows what on the world, which could in turn create such havoc, the world as you know it in Ebenezer Falls will end."

Man, did my stomach take a dive for the ground then. "So just to get this guy off my back, I have to risk my town?"

Atti's tiny eyes, normally direct, skittered over my shoulder. "Possibly, but there's a real percentage of a chance that won't happen, Stephania."

"I won't let it happen, Stevie. *I'll protect you*," Hal urged.

I threw my hands up in the air in helplessness. It was one thing to risk my life, but the entirety of Eb Falls? My family, my friends. *No.* "That's a ten as far as I'm concerned. Let's just give him what he wants. Call him out, I'll hand myself over, and we're done."

"Dove!" Win barked in unison with Hal, who bellowed my name. "There is absolutely no way I would ever let that happen, beloved. Where you go, I go."

I looked down at the floor, my eyes tearing up. He was always so gallant and I knew he meant what he said. But... "It's not your choice, Win," I responded quietly.

"Enough!" Atti growled. "When—*if*—his essence arrives in that portal, we shall capture him in that box, laden heavily with magic, where he can never trouble anyone again, and I won't hear otherwise. Understood?"

We both nodded with reluctance as though we'd been scolded by a superior.

Taking deep breaths, I ran my finger over the parchment scroll with the diagram, unrolling it. My eyes widened at yet another roadblock. "Is da Vinci coming along for the ride, because I flunked art and this looks pretty complicated."

"Indeed," Win agreed. "That is incredibly complex, Atticus."

"Magic, Stephania," Atticus reminded sharply. "We shall use magic to draw the diagram on the ground."

"Right. Magic. By the deciduous tree in some unknown location while we open a portal to who knows where and maybe blow up the world," I said on a shaky breath.

Hal grabbed my hand. "It's okay, Stevie. I'll be right there with you. I swear, I would never leave you. We're in it till the end."

Boy, had I gotten lucky when Hal found me. "Excuse me, but when did you get so confidant? This is a big, scary deal, Hal."

She shook her head in the negative with a grim smile. "I'm not confidant at all. I'm terrified, but I know someone who once told me to always face your attacker like you're the biggest baddie in the land.

Never let 'em see ya sweat. I'm just following your advice."

I should just learn to keep my big mouth shut. What did I know anyway? I'm a wannabe sleuth who can't keep her nose out of a good mystery who happens to see ghosts and now, occasionally hears them. Why am I giving advice to anyone? I shouldn't be allowed to advise a rock.

Win cupped my chin. "She's right, Mini-Spy, and I'll be there, too. No matter what."

"Me, too, *malutka. Always.*"

Tears sprang to my eyes, but I didn't have time to indulge in them because my phone pinged with an incoming text.

I smiled. As terrified as I was, Sandwich was at the door, asking for advice on the cute new girl who worked at the beauty salon. He'd been wanting to ask her out, but he was nervous, and I told him if he needed to talk, all he had to do was say the word.

Plus, I could use a moment to clear my head. "You guys start figuring this out and who's doing what. Sandwich is at the door. Girl troubles. I'll only be a sec."

Hal was up and on her feet in an instant. "I'll go with," she said.

I waved her off. "Don't be silly. It's just Sandwich."

"Is it?" she asked, and that was fair.

"Fine, Bodyguard," I teased. "Follow me." I padded out of the kitchen and down the hall to the front door. Popping it open, I smiled at Sandwich before turning to Hal. "See? It's just Sandwich. Aw, buddy, you look a little beaten down."

Right then and there, like a bolt of lightning, two things happened.

I finally remembered where I'd heard someone say they wanted me battered and soulless.

I believe the words were, *I want you dead, Stevie Cartwright. I want you broken, battered, beaten, begging for mercy, and then I want you dead.*

And number two?

Hal was right.

It wasn't just Sandwich.

CHAPTER 17

I woke with a start. A painful one—one where I couldn't remember what had happened to me until I realized I was freezing cold and soaking wet. Snow pelted my face and my eyeball felt like it might fall right out of my head from throbbing.

Looking around to get my bearings, I realized I was sitting on the ground, tied to a tree trunk. A big tree trunk. Maybe even a deciduous one, huh? I don't know why that made me want to giggle, but there you have it. With my luck, it was the wrong deciduous tree, but for sure, I was in a forest somewhere, much like the one Hal described in her vision. Peering into the curtain of thick snow, I oriented myself.

A groan escaped my lips when I finally found what I was looking for.

Sandwich.

Likely possessed by Sal.

If I've said it once, I'll say it again, what's happened

to the afterlife and how are people—especially someone like Sal, who'd come across as an utter dolt when he was alive—hopping bodies and in general, creating mayhem without possessing so much as a shred of the kind of moxie Win had? Win fought long and hard to get here, and Sal was skipping around all over the place willy-nilly with nary a care.

How had he gotten me from Hal and, worse, how was I going to save myself if no one knew where I was and I had but a smidge of unreliable magic?

Swallowing hard, my throat still sore from my encounter with Juan Felipe and my head pounding, I tried to straighten my spine so I could face my stalker like a big girl.

Where the heck was I? For all I knew, as crafty as Sal had become, maybe I was in the Alps, high atop a mountain.

At the moment, Sal was busying himself moving some sort of altar around. There were rocks piled high in a semi-circle, covered in newly fallen snow, with a large pit in the middle of them.

Instantly, I knew what he was going to do. I'd heard about it before, but it was a rare ritual, and as witches, one we all thought mostly just rumors. Though, all of the things I'd been taught were rare didn't appear so rare these days. So I might as well throw the rule book on rare out the window and go with anything really *was* possible.

Anyway, in case you're wondering, he's going to sacrifice my soul for Sandwich's body—a body he can keep forever. I'm not sure of the logistics of getting into the body. Killing me would be easy, but if I'm not mistaken, much like the evocation spell, there were specifics to when he killed me and how and blah, blah, blah.

Oddly, despite the fact that I was freezing cold, my teeth were chattering, my hands were numb and I was tied up, I felt freakishly calm.

Thus, I figured it was time to address the elephant in the room…er, forest. "Ahem," I said, clearing my throat. "Hey, Sal. Long time no see. How ya been?"

He turned around, moving surprisingly quickly. He'd adjusted to Sandwich's body with no problem at all.

And then he laughed, deep and very unlike Sandwich, tipping his head back so the snow fell on his throat and face.

Also, his laugh was very unlike Sal's, too…

"If it isn't little Stevie Cartwright. Woebegone witch with no powers and buckets full of money. I'm doing all right, Stevie. I see you've been well since we last met."

As he spoke, I fought my gasp of shock when I remembered I had figured out who the culprit was just before I'd been spirited away—and it wasn't Sal Finch.

As my own stupidity washed over me at how I'd been completely played for a gosh darn fool all this time, I refused to show my surprise or my terror.

Instead, I said with a grin, "Well, well, well. As I live and breathe. If it isn't Adam Westfield. What happened, buddy? Too afraid to handle me on your own, so you found yourself a bunch of lackeys to do your dirty work, did you? You've been a busy boy."

His laughter, deep and demonic, rumbling out of Sandwich's mouth, made my stomach roil with bile. Sandwich, who was as sweet as pecan pie and kind as the day was long, had this insidious monster inside him, and if this monster won, he'd kill off not only my soul, but Sandwich's, too.

How did I miss that it was Adam all this time? How could I have missed the signs? How did we all miss the signs?

Were there signs? My mind reeled, replaying the last couple of days.

Adam rolled his eyes as the snow plastered his hair to his head and his round face glistened. "You know, I bet you're thinking, why didn't I figure out it was my old buddy Adam Westfield possessing bodies and sending flower bombs?"

If he only knew. "I'll admit it," I said from chattering teeth. "You had me fooled. I totally believed it was Sal Finch, hunting me. Bravo, you."

He curtsied awkwardly, Sandwich's big body bending at the knees, his grin, once innocent and vulnerable and exactly the reason Adam had picked him, now filled with malevolence.

"Why, thank you, madam. I took a little while to choose who I'd pretend to be. I mean, so many people hate your guts because you don't know how to mind your own business, but Sal felt right, yanno? He's sleazy enough to do something like this."

He paused for a moment and looked at me long and hard through Sandwich's kind eyes. Then he said, "But you know what I can't figure out? Whatever made you think he was smart enough to accomplish something like this? What made you think he had the longevity and the stamina to pull something like this off? "

I wrung my hands against the zip ties that held my wrists behind my back, rubbing my skin raw, hoping to loosen them and wondering the same stupid thing.

Though, I think I should still get points for questioning Sal's intelligence. I just never guessed it was Adam. He'd been gone for so long, he'd become a distant nightmare.

But obviously, he'd spent some time in the afterlife, honing his skills.

"Ya got me there, too, Adam. I really did fall for the show you put on. Hook, line and sinker. We all did. All that in and out of bodies and conning people into doing things they wouldn't normally do. You're really smart. It must be the genius in you. You did your homework, huh?"

At those words, he rushed at me so fast, I thought he might crash into me, pushing his way through the mounds of snow with force.

Instead, he dropped to his knees and grabbed me by the collar of my shirt with his beefy hands and gave me a shake that rattled my very bones and slammed my head back against the tree.

At this rate, my melon was going to end up with brain damage for all the smashing around it had taken today.

"Shut up, you stupid cow! Don't you mock me! You ruined my life!"

I yawned right in his face. Right in Sandwich's sweet, gentle face. I think I'd waited for this day for a long time. For the time when it was just me and Adam, facing off so we could end this one way or the other. And if the end meant my end, too, so be it. I was ready to unburden this cloud hanging over me, always there, always leaving me looking over my shoulder.

"Yeah, yeah, and mine was a real laugh riot. I was shunned and booted from my coven and I lost all my powers. All you did was die, you slovenly pig," I spat. "That was the easy way out, and you deserved it, you child-abuser!"

I saw a confused look pass over his face. Sandwich was in there somewhere. Sandwich would die before hurting anything, least of all a child. He was inherently good, and if I knew my Sandwich, he would try his hardest to fight the evil that had consumed him.

Which gave me an idea. Maybe I could reach him. Maybe Sandwich was stronger than I'd ever given him credit for...

But then Adam's expression hardened again and he shook me rougher. "But you landed on your feet, didn't you, Stevie. You with your house and your British tattletale, skipping through life as though there's nothing but rainbows at the end of the road. You will pay for what you did to me, for what you did to my family!" he roared, spittle forming at the corners of his mouth.

He didn't only enrage me, he terrified me. I was terrified of this man who'd ruined my life.

But what Hal had said to me before I was taken by Sandwich came back to me tenfold—words I had shared with her. *Never let 'em see you sweat,* and while I might die for it, I was leaving Win, my sister, Bel, and everyone I loved in my life kicking and screaming the whole way.

"Will I, Adam?" I screeched, straining at the rope he'd tied me to the tree with. "If you say so then do it, you panty waste! Be a man and do it. Kill me. Take my soul. Batter and beat me until I'm nothing but skin and bones. Let's dance, you filthy pig! You took my powers from me because you got *caught,* wife-beater! You're spiteful and filled with ugly hatred, and now you'll steal someone's body to take your revenge and go on beating women. How's your wife, Anne, going to feel about that? Will you go back to her like a bad little boy with his tail between his legs, or will you find some other poor, unsuspecting woman to beat black and blue?"

That stopped him in his tracks, but only for a moment before he said, his voice low and eerily intimidating, "I'm good, Stevie, but I'm not that good. Who do you think helped me build the bomb?"

His wife? His wife had helped him build a bomb?

I had to fight with every single bit of energy I had to keep from gasping out loud.

Then the letters *WIF* smacked me in the face. Tito had been trying to spell *wife*. He'd been trying to warn me that Adam's wife, Anne, was helping him.

Son of a cheddar bay biscuit.

And that made me angry. Made me hate him more than I ever had before—because I'd bet my teeth she didn't help him because she wanted to. She'd helped him because she was afraid of him, intimidated and terrorized by him.

That thought made me cocky. "Did you beat her into submission so she'd do it, Adam? You know, the way you did when you talked her into telling the council and Baba Yaga what a good husband you were? The same way you frightened your son so much, he went along with her story? Is that what you did?"

He pulled his big palm back and let 'er rip, slapping me almost as hard as he had the day he'd stolen my powers.

Yet the sting and the heat of my freshly struck face almost felt good compared to the freezing cold.

So I jammed my face in his to show him there was nothing left in me to take. "Slap away, you ape! There's nothing else you can take from me. Nothing you haven't already taken. My powers are gone. Beat me until I'm battered and bruised and nothing but a shell of my former self. Go on, coward. Do! It!"

Now he hauled me up close to him by the collar of

my shirt, pulling the restraints on my wrists so tight, I thought they might cut off my hands.

"Shut your face! Shut it or I'll rip it off!"

I searched his eyes, at first cloudy, but for a moment bright and alert. "Sandwich. *Lyn*…listen to me. It's Stevie. Your friend. I know you must be afraid. I know you don't understand what's happening. I know you're in there. But don't be afraid. I'm with you. Fight him, Sandwich. Fight him as hard as you can!"

For a millisecond, he looked at me. Afraid, alone, with eyes that almost teared up…and then they glazed over again, hard as ice chips and Adam returned.

"Do you really think this tub of lard is stronger than me, Stevie?" He laughed the words. "Don't be absurd!" he bellowed in my face before he slammed me back against the trunk of the tree and stomped back off to the altar.

Goddess and all her wisdom, I couldn't remember what he had to do to get my soul from me, I couldn't remember the ritual, but I did know it would be painful—and I had a decision to make.

Inflict Adam on the world or save myself.

He was too smart to let himself be riled into anything rash, that much was obvious after I'd taunted him. Clearly, timing was crucial.

Think, Stevie, think!

My father! No one had been able to reach him on whatever remote shoot he was on, but I had the necklace he'd given me around my neck. If I could only get my hands loose enough to touch it to call upon him, maybe he could help.

It was then I felt small feet on my shoulder and heard, "Boss, it's me."

A cold slither of fear ran along my arms and spine. "Bel?"

"And I," Atti said.

"Are you two insane?" I whispered as they burrowed into my hair to hide. "How did you find me?"

"Apparently, witch GPS is a real thing and that compass is the bomb," Bel whispered back.

Fear sliced through my veins. "Go back. Get out. It's not Sal. It's Adam. He'll kill you both!"

"Shhh, pet. Listen. Listen well. Halliday and Win are here. In the shrubs to the north with the box. You must heed my words. Adam Westfield is not impervious to losing his own soul. We can capture it in the box, but it must be the right time. It must be a precise removal."

My chest heaved and my heart thrashed. "And how am I going to do that without magic?"

"You have the magic, Stephania," Atti insisted. "*You must believe.* You must trust me when I tell you that you can do this. Halliday will help. Now listen closely. Look up to the sky."

I did as I was told and saw nothing but clouds.

"When the clouds clear, when the moon shines down upon the small clearing to your left, you must say these words. '*Goddess of purity and light, take this soul, make this right. Evil lives upon our plane. It must be banished, to stop the pain.*'"

This felt like the third grade play, where I played a talking head of cabbage (of all things) in *Peter Rabbit*, but because I sucked at remembering lines no matter how much I practiced, I flubbed them and ran off the stage in embarrassment.

"Do you see what he's doing, Atti?"

Never one to mince words, he said in his direct nature, "Yes, poppet. He's preparing a pit to bury your body in with hemlock and nightshade in order to ensure your soul will evaporate and go through the portal."

Panic seized me by the throat. "He's opening a portal, too?"

I felt Atti shift, his body language telling me he didn't want to add to my misery, when he reluctantly said, "Yes."

Desperation took hold as I squirmed, blood dripping from my wrists, my face soaking wet. "So two portals for the price of one? How are we going to stop this, Atti?"

"We won't allow that to happen, Stephania. We'll open the one he must leave this plane through in that box before he has the chance to open another. *We will.*"

If I was defiantly spitting in the face of fear a few moments ago, now I was cowering against the trunk of this tree, wet, cold, miserable and terrified. "Oh, sure, easy for you to say. You have magic. Why can't you and Hal just stop it?"

I hated that I sounded like such a chicken, but all I'd done so far was freeze people in place and blow a door up. I didn't have their kind of magic.

"Because we need the power of three and no one else wants to help, Boss! So cut the crap! Your magic *is* coming back. When Atti says it, I believe him. Are you gonna let this douche of canoes win and kill you, or are you going to get it together and at least try?"

The power of three. I'd heard of it. Three magical beings to save one soul—mine. Bel was right. I had to get it together.

I had to. *I would.*

"And the diagram?" I whispered against the howl of the icy wind.

"I'll handle the diagram to produce the portal," Atti assured me.

Instantly, I took deep breaths, inhaling cold snow and frigid air. Sitting up straight again, I tried to remember the spell to release myself from a binding so my hands would be loose and I stood a fighting chance.

Closing my eyes, I whispered, "Release me binds that hold. Release me, please, I ask so bold."

"Bloody well done, Stephania!" Atti whispered fiercely when the ties loosened enough and I jerked forward.

I sat stunned for a moment, but only a moment when I realized I had no time to pat myself on the back. What I had to do was pretend to still be tied to the tree. My arms ached and my chest hurt from the tug of the binds, but I kept them there while Adam dug the hole, dirt and snowy debris flying everywhere.

"Now what?" I said in hushed tones.

"Wait, Stephania. You wait. The high moon is nigh. When I say now, you speak the words."

"Have I told you I suck at remembering stuff like

that?" I asked, blood dripping down my hands. "Ask Bel about my third-grade school play."

"We'll stay right here on your shoulder, Boss. I'll help you say them just like I did in third grade. I'll never leave your side."

"But you *did* leave my side. You slept through my third-grade play," I reminded in a whisper-yell.

"Okay, okay, I'm not perfect, but I'm here now and I'll never leave your side again. Not ever. If you go into that portal, I go with."

My heart clenched so tight, I thought it would burst. "I love you, Bel. Remember that. Always. But if you don't save yourself, I'll borrow someone else's soul and haunt you for eternity."

"Hush and look up," Atti demanded.

I looked up at the sky and noted a small swoosh of the clouds parting, dancing against the midnight-black sky. The moon would be visible soon.

What felt like forever was likely only two or three minutes, but suddenly, Adam stopped what he was doing and looked in my direction.

I narrowed my eyes at him and pretended to struggle against the ties.

"Oh, Stevie," he called out with a hateful chuckle. "I can't wait to see the look on your face when I ship you off to nothingness. I feel like I've waited forever for this moment."

He went back to what he was doing, and that was when I saw Win, just across the clearing, behind some kind of snow-covered bush, his beautiful face chiseled, his eyes burning holes in mine, his stare was so intent. *"I love you, Dove. Forever,"* he mouthed.

Somehow, it gave me the strength I needed when Atti whispered in my ear, "Now, Stephania, bloody well *now!*"

Popping up from the tree, my legs creaking when I pushed the rope off me as Hal came running from the bush in the clearing, snow spitting up behind her, that infernal box in her hand.

We somehow managed to sync our words and, together with Atti, we screamed into the clearing, *"Goddess of purity and light, take this soul, make this right. Evil lives upon our plane. It must be banished, to stop the pain!"*

Adam's head popped up as he looked around, his head swiveling left and right while we came at him from all sides.

I ran straight for him. All the heartache, all the pain, all the humiliation and rage I'd had inside me for all these years let loose—as though I were freed from some prison.

I ran with abandon, screaming the words again. "Goddess of purity and light, take this soul, make this right. Evil lives upon our plane. It must be banished, to stop the pain!"

At first, he didn't budge. He dropped the shovel and stood there under the moonlight, shimmering and shifting.

Then he lifted his hand and a bolt of lightning fell

from the sky, scorching the ground in front of me and stopping me cold.

"You didn't think I'd be stupid enough to think you wouldn't call upon your waste of a witch sister for help, did you, Stevie?" he yelled over the roar of thunder.

I sucked in the cold air as Hal stopped dead, too, while Win crept around behind Adam and hid in the trees, likely hoping for a sneak attack.

When we said nothing as the scorched earth burned, even on the cold, wet snow, Adam continued. "That's why I brought insurance." He snapped his fingers and Karen appeared out of thin air. Bound by rope, her eyes flashing and angry.

"Nana?" I heard Hal cry out, and it tore at my heart.

"Let her go, Adam! She has nothing to do with this!" I yelled, pushing my soaking-wet hair from my face, my fingers raw and almost blue.

"But she does," he cackled. "She means something to you, just like my life meant something to me. You took that away. Now I'll take *all* of them away because they mean something to you!" He shoved Karen toward the blazing ground.

I heard her cry out, "You SOB! You're gonna wish you'd killed me when I get done with you, you hear me? Girls, run—go! *Go now!*"

Not on your life—er…reincarnated life.

"Shut up!" he hollered at Karen, shoving her onto her back where she lay helpless like a fish out of water, her hooves in the air, her antlers smacking against the snow.

Instead of responding. Instead of further taunting him, I decided to give him what he wanted.

I'm not sure where Atti got this spell of his. Maybe it was a cereal box or some shady witch sold him a bill of goods, but Adam wasn't budging and the spell sucked monkey poop. II didn't see any portal.

And I wasn't going to let him hurt people I loved to the very depth of my being while I waited for it to show up.

I held up my hands, my wrists bloody and raw, and began walking toward him, tears streaming down my face. "Let them all go and I'll get in the hole without another word."

"Stephania!" Atti pecked at my ear. "Do not give in! You must wait and believe!"

But I didn't listen. I stepped around the fire, going to Karen to roll her over to a more comfortable position. "Don't give up, Stevie. Don't you dare!" she said with a hiss.

I ignored her, too. My life wasn't worth everyone else's in return. We didn't all have to go down with the ship.

"I mean it, Adam," I said on a shaky breath as I got closer and closer to my doomed fate. "Take me, but leave everyone else alone—and I swear to you, if you hurt any of them after you take my soul, I'll find a way to make you suffer in the same way you did to me."

"Stephania, no!" Win yelled, rushing out from

behind a tree, but I shook my head. I had no tricks up my sleeve, nothing else to offer to sweeten the pot.

"I love you, Win. You're the best thing that's ever happened to me," I said, choking out the words as I sat at the edge of the hole, the cold ground permeating my wet clothes again. I scooped up Atti and Bel in my palm and hurled them into the sky, where they fluttered their wings. "Stay with Win. He'll need you, Bel."

And then I looked up at Adam in Sandwich's body. He cocked his head, likely thinking I was bluffing, but I wasn't. "Do it, Adam! Go on! Do it, you coward!"

"Stevie, nooo!" I heard Hal scream, her voice raw with emotion as she ran toward me. "*No!*"

I held up my hand to thwart her, and by some miracle, she froze.

Huh.

It was then that I felt something in me surge, something pulse to life and beat like that of a heart. It whooshed upward throughout my body, spreading through my limbs, making my toes tingle as lightning cracked and thunder roared.

And then there were faces all around me. Ghosts from my past, ghosts I'd crossed over, ghosts I'd helped…

And Arkady. My treasured friend Arkady, in the middle of them all, leading them the way I imagine he led his spies when he was alive.

They all began to chant over and over, "*Goddess of purity and light, take this soul, make this right. Evil lives upon this plane. It must be banished, to stop the pain!*"

Adam fell backward in surprise, stumbling and tripping over Karen as we all began to chant and the strength of ten men filled my body. I rose and began walking toward him as he crab-walked backward in the snow, rising to his feet to shoot bolts of lighting, leaving a path of fire in his wake.

Yet, I plowed forward, repeating the words until we were eye to eye.

"I'll kill you!" he raged before he began to turn away —to run from me.

Adam Westfield was running from me.

Well, well.

But I wasn't letting him get away this time. Not this time.

As the voices rose around me, I ran after him, my frozen feet like blocks of ice, tackling him in the snow.

We hit the ground with a *thunk* and a crack of bones, puffs of snow flying up in the air. But he was strong, rising on sturdy feet. I wrapped my legs around his bulky waist as tight as I could, he grabbed me by the throat, lifting his hand high in the air, preparing to knock me square in the face again.

"Not this time, you filthy pig!" I screamed, raising my hand, too, and with all my might, I slapped him in the face.

I slapped him so hard, my hand stung and my frozen fingers crackled. A slap so harsh, the crack echoed throughout the snow-covered forest.

He backed up in surprise and fell, taking me with

him where we again landed in the snow, covered in blood and soaking wet.

I don't know where it came from. I don't have any explanation for how I knew my next words. All I could think was, *Believe, Stevie. You must believe.*

I straddled him and grabbed him by the collar of his shirt, hauling him upward with bloody fingers and screeched in his face, "Be gone your soul, Adam Westfield, be gone forever! Be gone pure evil. Be gone, to return never!"

Adam shook beneath me as though an earthquake was surging the forest floor, his body trembling and quaking violently. A hole with a bright light appeared, howls and screeches filled the interior, flames licked at the opening—and then I saw him.

Adam Westfield's face, filled with surprised rage, with hate, with his insidious brand of sickness, and all I could think was that I wanted him out of my sweet Sandwich's body. I couldn't let him have Sandwich.

So I slapped him again for good measure, this time with Hal standing by and Win at her side, box open. I slapped him so hard, I left an imprint of my hand on his face. "I owe you one, Adam! I owe you one!" I howled.

The earth began to crumble beneath us, but I held on tight until a wisp of smoke rose from Sandwich's body, a stench so odious, we all gagged.

The moment Adam's soul left Sandwich's body, Atti yelled from above, "Capture him in the box, Halliday, and throw it in the portal! Time is of the essence."

Hal swooped in and grabbed at the smoke with the open box, slamming the top shut and running with it like a linebacker heading for a goal.

She lobbed it into the portal seconds before it closed and swallowed Adam Westfield whole, his screams of agony echoing all around us.

I slumped forward against Sandwich's chest, exhausted, praying to the universe that he was unharmed. I ran my hands over his face, feeling the difference in his aura, knowing instinctually it was him.

"Sandwich! Oh, my friend, say you're okay," I whispered against his round cheek.

"Stevie?" he said, hoarse and low. "Why are you sitting on my chest? Win won't like that, and besides, I like someone else. I already told you that."

I sat up and began to laugh, laugh so hard my stomach hurt as Sandwich stared up at me in confusion, his uniform muddy and torn, his eyes bright and clear.

Hal kneeled down and gave him a warm smile. "Sandwich, I'm Hal. Close your eyes."

But I put my hand on my sister's arm. "I've got this." Putting my fingertips over his eyes, I closed them. "Close your eyes, Sandwich, all will be right. Back to your warm bed, rest well for the night."

He disappeared from beneath me, leaving me in a heap on the ground, but Win was there to scoop me up. He opened his down jacket and pulled me to him so tight, I almost couldn't breathe.

"Don't you ever do that to me again, Stephania! Do you understand? There will be no sacrifices for my life. Never, ever!"

I threw my arms around him and hugged him tight. I was freezing cold, bloody, a little beat up, but I'd done it. "I swear, I'll never sacrifice my life for yours ever again," I said, softly kissing his cheek…with my fingers crossed.

"That said, beloved—you did it!" He swung me around, setting me back on my feet. "I'm gathering your magic is back? You were incredible!"

"Dah, *malutka*. I have seen many things in my time, but never do I see a woman as strong as you."

"Thank you, Arkady. It was you who convinced everyone to come, wasn't it?"

"Bah! It was not hard. Arkady Bagrov can be very charming when he wants. But everyone want to help, my buttery poundcake. All the people you help want to help you. You make me proud, warrior. So proud to call you friend."

"I love you," I whispered upward to him. "I love you all. Thank you. I'll never be able to repay your kindness."

Hal snorted from behind Win. "Oh, I think now that you have your powers back, they're gonna come calling a whole lot more."

I stepped out of Win's arms and grabbed my sister, hugging her hard. "You're one of the best things to ever happen to me. I love you, Halliday Valentine. Thank you for believing when I couldn't."

Even in the moonlight, I could see her cheeks turn red. "Yeah, yeah. Now, let's go home. I'm cold, you're soaking wet, and there's a bottle of something fancy in your fridge that Win thinks he's been hiding from me. We're gonna pop that cork and celebrate. You didn't just get that monkey off your back, you got your magic back."

That made me stop for a second as we walked back toward the clearing. "Your vision! You said I was a husk and my soul was gone." I froze for a moment. "Is that still going to happen?"

"You turned into a husk…but not because you were dead. Because you were being reborn. It only became clear to me when I saw you slap Adam. You got your magic back, Stevie. You took your power back from him."

I bit the inside of my cheek. "Huh. Crazy, right?"

We began walking again, Hal and Win on either side of me, when Bel called out, buzzing to my shoulder, "Hey, Boss. Does this mean no more icebergs in the backyard?"

Hal's eyes opened wide. "You made an iceberg in the backyard?"

"It was a long time ago, and my familiar just can't seem to let it go. My magic kept coming back in blips and spurts and all I got was an iceberg."

Win wrapped his arm around my waist. "Don't forget the dinosaur, Dove. That was quite spectacular."

Atti scoffed. "Hah! Halliday made a dragon appear."

Hal winced. "It's true. I'm glad your magic came

back. Who knows where we'd be right now. When I'm stressed or nervous, it gets a little weird."

I stopped again, looking around. "Karen! Where's Karen?"

"I sent her back. She's eating candy canes and lovin' life. She's fine."

I sighed in relief and squeezed Hal's hand. "Question?"

Hal looked at me, her blue eyes intense. "Uh-huh?"

"Why are we walking?"

"Yeah. Why *are* we walking?" she asked as she raised her fingers to snap them.

But I stopped her. "Nope. I got this."

I snapped my fingers and thought about home. We landed safely back in the entryway, dripping wet and greeted by Whiskey and Strike.

Like I said, I got this.

Boy did I ever.

Three days later...

We sat with Baba Yaga at our kitchen table. She'd come the moment I said I was ready to see her, in all her '80s glory.

I stared down at my coffee cup as the snow fell and Win sat silent, holding my hand for support. I wasn't sure I wanted to see her, but now that I was officially a witch again, I didn't really have a choice.

Hal and Atti had taken their leave earlier this morning, and I'd thanked them over and over for their support when no one else had been there to help me.

We made plans to see each other soon, and I sent an entire case of candy canes to Karen to make up for her kidnapping.

Now I was faced with my reckoning, coming to terms with my new powers and having to deal with all that entailed.

After Baba explained a few things to me about

Adam Westfield, and Winnie, who had no idea what was going on or she would have come no matter what Baba said, I was finally able to speak, but my words were neither warm nor forgiving.

"So basically, you dumped me to keep Adam Westfield in check?" I asked, her beautifully flawless face pained at the question.

"Oh, my sweet summer child," Baba replied warmly. "There was no other way. Don't you think if I could have done something, I would have? Can I tell you how much it's hurt me…your hatred?"

I gave her a defiant look and Win squeezed my hand. "Don't guilt trip me. That's unfair."

"You're right, Stephania. Just know, could it have been any other way, I would have made it so. I did what was best for the greater good."

I softened a little then. "I didn't hate you, BY. I just didn't like you much. You took everything away from me. My coven, my home, my job. It hurt."

She spread her arms wide. "But look what you have now, precious. Look at this life you've built. It's magnificent, and so is your young man."

I clenched my sore jaw till my teeth almost cracked. I'd promised Win I would listen, and I had.

"If what you've come to tell me is I have to go back to Texas, you can forget it. I'm not leaving here, Baba. I don't care about the coven or how strong it is because I'm suddenly the witchiest witch in the land. You were all just fine without me. You don't need me to keep our circle strong. I'm not leaving my home—my life.

Ebenezer Falls is where I belong, with Win and Belfry, Arkady, Whiskey and Strike."

According to Baba, I'm a force to be reckoned with. I'm apparently, now that I've defeated the evilest warlock ever, the strongest witch in the land.

When I slapped Adam, my powers didn't just return—his came with mine. I'd *always* had my powers, and that's why they kept slipping through—but Baba had squelched them to keep me safe.

At least, that was her story.

She reached out and cupped my sore face. "I can't ask that of you, but I also can't say that I don't wish you'd reconsider. The coven's missed you."

I scoffed and looked out the window. "Yeah, they missed me so much, they turned their backs on me and left me to my own devices." I was still feeling pretty grudgy at this point, but Baba softened further.

She gripped my hand and squeezed it. "To protect them and their families, Stevie. Any information they had could hurt them. I had *everyone* to consider."

Gosh, that sting of being shunned was still there. It wasn't as strong, but it ached a little. "Is this going to be the old, 'this hurt me more than it hurt you' talk? Collateral damage. Because it *did* hurt, Baba. I can't tell you how much it hurt."

Her eyes searched mine. "I'd rather you hurt than your soul stolen. If I suppressed your powers, Adam couldn't find you, but it wasn't easy, Stevie. You're a powerful warrior—one that made me so proud. But he was *more* powerful. So powerful, I couldn't contain him. The council couldn't contain him. No one could, and his vendetta against you was one like I've never seen in my many years on this plane. He wanted you ruined, Stevie. Because of that, I made decisions I don't regret. Like banishing you from the coven."

I cocked my head in confusion. "But he still found me, Baba. He fought with my mother right out there in my front yard. He possessed an innocent human."

"He found you *because* of Dita and your father. You know we can smell another witch, Stevie. He smelled their magic—that's how he found you the first time. After that all-out war in the front yard with your mother where she really walloped him, we thought we'd found a way to contain him and his spirit. We even used a containment spell to keep him away from you."

Holy spit, that was the biggest of big spells I knew of. "But obviously that didn't work because he got to Edmund."

She sighed with a rasp of frustration. "Oh, it did for a while, and then it didn't. Then he kidnapped Belfry and possessed that poor boy, and then he disappeared and no one knew where he was. He hid himself well, my friend. He plane hopped, frightening the spirits to the point of silence. He worked long and hard to achieve that level of evil, bartered, threatened, pushed and shoved until he was capable of more than any entity I've ever seen."

"Surprise," I said sarcastically. "Might have been

nice to tell me no one knew where he was and his vendetta for me was so sick."

Baba's look was one of pure guilt. "Again, the less you knew the better. I thought we could contain him. We didn't know he was missing until last night—*after* your battle with him. I'm so sorry I was wrong."

"So all this time, I've had my powers—all these years you just squashed them? Suppressed them and left me to fend for myself?"

"Yep, kiddo, but they managed to find their way to the surface no matter what I did. You're a beast. Oh, Stephania...I knew you'd find your way back here. I knew you'd make a life for yourself and Belfry. You were strong even without your powers. If anyone could start over, it was you."

I turned my eyes back to the window and watched the snow fall. "So now what? What do you want from me?"

Baba put her hand on my bruised back and gently caressed with her palm, wiping away my aches. "Nothing, Stevie. Nothing you don't want to do, but if you ever wanted to come back to Texas to visit—maybe even stay—we'd welcome you with open arms and wide-open hearts."

"I don't know if I'm ready for that yet," I whispered. "I don't know if I ever will be. I still feel betrayed."

"Stevie, I know you think I did this to punish you, but it was done out of love and my deep need to keep you safe."

"But what about everyone else? My entire coven

shunned me. Everyone but Winnie. How can I ever trust them again?"

"Because they did what they were told to do, Stevie. Because they had your back," Baba Yaga said softly. "Not all of the coven agreed. In fact, Winnie vehemently *disagreed*. She thought we could keep you safe, but there were some things I couldn't tell her about the severity of Adam's powers and his vendetta, for her safety as well. No one could know what was going on behind the scenes. So in the end, we all agreed you had to be kept safe. *You* were our priority."

It all made sense, but I needed time to process it. "I don't know when I'll be ready," I whispered. "I need time to absorb everything you've told me."

Baba rose and straightened her blazer with padded shoulders to smile warmly at me. "You take all the time you need, Stevie Cartwright. We'll always be there—even if it's just for a visit."

She was about to take her leave when I hopped up from the table and impulsively gave her a hug—one she returned tenfold. "Maybe I'll see you soon," I whispered, relishing the scent of her perfume and her warm embrace, even if I didn't want to admit it comforted me.

"I hope so, sweet girl. I hope so." She squeezed me one last time and she was gone, leaving Win and I alone at the table with our coffee and danish.

After a while, Win said, "Dove? Tell me how you feel, won't you?"

I sipped my coffee and considered that question as I

looked at his handsome face. "I guess I don't know. After being so angry for so long, then finally learning to live my life without the crutch of my anger, and now having it all back again, it's…it's a lot."

"Of course it is, but might I share something with you?"

I smiled at him, my eyeball still a little sore when my cheeks lifted. "Of course."

"I spent a lot of my time as a spy reading people, and what I read from Baba was sincerity, devotion to taking care of *all* of you—of protecting you from harm. I know that's not what you want to hear, and while I'll always be on your side, I believe her words are true."

I blinked back tears. "I think I do, too. I just need some time to…adjust."

Win took a bite of his danish and nodded. "Take all the time you need. You deserve it." Then he gave me his quirky smile. "Question?"

"Answer," I responded with a grin.

"You were responsible for Amos Thorn's career?" Win said in awe.

I laughed. I wondered when that would come up. Win was a big fan. "Nah. Professor Tim was responsible. I just gave him the number for the publisher so she'd look at his manuscript and it wouldn't end up in the slush pile—or whatever it's called."

"He writes incredible medical thrillers. What a wonderful thing you've done, Dove. Proven by all those ghosts who showed up in that forest on your behalf."

I blushed, but I couldn't take credit. "I didn't do

anything but deliver a message. I'm glad the world got to share in his talent. Which reminds me..."

"Of," he asked with a raised eyebrow.

"You do realize, now that my powers have returned, I'm going to be busier than a one-toothed man in a corn-eating contest."

Win's head fell back on his shoulders in laughter before he held out his hand to me. "Does it make you happy, my beloved?"

"It does. It makes me feel even more useful than I do at Madame Z's. As though I have a purpose again. A bigger purpose, anyway."

"Then you chat with all the ghosts you like. I'm happy to help where I can."

I winced. "I just remembered, you can hear them, too. It's going to be a madhouse."

"Hah!" he barked with a slap of his hand to the table. "When hasn't it been a madhouse? We don't call this Mayhem Manor for nothing."

I'd forgotten we used to joke about the house when it was still in its reno stages. "That's true, but I have years' worth of catching up to do. You ready for that?"

He grabbed my hand and kissed my fingertips. "I'm ready for whatever you bring. As long as I'm with you."

As long as I'm with you...

Words every girl loves to hear.

"Always," I said, my throat tight.

"Very good," he said, sitting up and releasing my hand. "Now, shall we address the elephant in the room?"

"The elephant?"

"Yes, Dove. Can't you hear it?"

I paused and held my breath before turning around and scanning the room. "What are you talking about?"

"Literally, there's an elephant in the room," he said on a chuckle and pointed over his shoulder.

Sure enough, there was a man with an elephant in the room, and as I listened closer, the elephant trumpeted a happy sound.

"And so it begins," I teased as I stood up and approached the man and his big friend.

Win rose, too, brushing nonexistent crumbs from his crisp trousers, his face handsome in the morning light. "Hashtag Stewin forever," he teased with a smile.

My heart glowed—literally glowed inside my chest. "Hashtag Stewin... *forever.*"

The End

NOTE FROM DAKOTA CASSIDY

I do hope you enjoyed this book, I'd so appreciate it if you'd help others enjoy it too.

Recommend it. Please help other readers find this book by recommending it.

Review it. Please tell other readers why you liked this book by reviewing it at online retailers or your blog. Reader reviews help my books continue to be valued by distributors/resellers. I adore each and every reader who takes the time to write one!

If you love the book or leave a review, thank you. Your support means more than you'll ever know! Thank you!

ABOUT THE AUTHOR

Dakota Cassidy is a USA Today bestselling author with over eighty books. She writes laugh-out-loud cozy mysteries, romantic comedy, grab-some-ice erotic romance, hot and sexy alpha males, paranormal shifters, contemporary kick-ass women, and more.

Dakota lives in the gorgeous state of Oregon with her real-life hero and her dogs, and she loves hearing from readers!

OTHER BOOKS BY DAKOTA CASSIDY

Visit Dakota's website at http://www. dakotacassidy.com for more information.

A Lemon Layne Mystery, a Contemporary Cozy Mystery Series

1. Prawn of the Dead
2. Play That Funky Music White Koi

Witchless In Seattle Mysteries, a Paranormal Cozy Mystery series

1. Witch Slapped
2. Quit Your Witchin'
3. Dewitched
4. The Old Witcheroo
5. How the Witch Stole Christmas
6. Ain't Love a Witch
7. Good Witch Hunting
8. Witch Way Did He Go?
9. Witches Get Stitches

10. Witch it Real Good
11. Witch Perfect
12. Gettin' Witched
13. Where There's a With, There's a Way
14. A Total Witch Show

Marshmallow Hollow Cozy Christmas Mysteries

1. Jingle All the Slay
2. Have Yourself a Merry Little Witness
3. One Corpse Open Slay

Nun of Your Business Mysteries, a Paranormal Cozy Mystery series

1. Then There Were Nun
2. Hit and Nun
3. House of the Rising Nun
4. The Smoking Nun
5. What a Nunderful World

Wolf Mates, a Paranormal Romantic Comedy series

1. An American Werewolf In Hoboken
2. What's New, Pussycat?
3. Gotta Have Faith
4. Moves Like Jagger
5. Bad Case of Loving You

A Paris, Texas Romance, a Paranormal Romantic Comedy series

1. Witched At Birth
2. What Not to Were
3. Witch Is the New Black
4. White Witchmas

Non-Series

Whose Bride Is She Anyway?

Polanski Brothers: Home of Eternal Rest
Sexy Lips 66
Accidentally Paranormal, a Paranormal Romantic Comedy series
Interview With an Accidental—a free introductory guide to the girls of the Accidentals!
1. The Accidental Werewolf
2. Accidentally Dead
3. The Accidental Human
4. Accidentally Demonic
5. Accidentally Catty
6. Accidentally Dead, Again
7. The Accidental Genie
8. The Accidental Werewolf 2: Something About Harry
9. The Accidental Dragon
10. Accidentally Aphrodite
11. Accidentally Ever After
12. Bearly Accidental
13. How Nina Got Her Fang Back
14. The Accidental Familiar
15. Then Came Wanda
16. The Accidental Mermaid
17. Marty's Horrible, Terrible Very Bad Day
18. The Accidental Unicorn
19. The Accidental Troll
20. Accidentally Divine
21. The Accidental Gargoyle
The Plum Orchard, a Contemporary Romantic Comedy series

1. Talk This Way
2. Talk Dirty to Me
3. Something to Talk About
4. Talking After Midnight

The Ex-Trophy Wives, a Contemporary Romantic Comedy series

1. You Dropped a Blonde On Me
2. Burning Down the Spouse
3. Waltz This Way

Fangs of Anarchy, a Paranormal Urban Fantasy series

1. Forbidden Alpha
2. Outlaw Alpha